Her Secret Beau

I0667792

Her Secret Beau

LEENIE BROWN

LEENIE B BOOKS
HALIFAX

Cover design by Leenie B Books. Images sourced from Deposit Photos and Period Images.

Her Secret Beau © 2019 Leenie Brown. All Rights Reserved, except where otherwise noted.

ISBN (print) 978-1-989410-48-6; (ebook) mobi: 978-1-989410-49-3

Contents

Dear Reader

This novel is part of my *Touches of Austen* Collection of Austenesque stories. These stories feature original characters and plots that have been touched in some way by the influence of Jane Austen and her novels.

As you read *Her Secret Beau*, you may notice nods to *Northanger Abbey*, *Persuasion*, *Sense and Sensibility*, and *Emma*. For instance, certain aspects of the heroine might make you think of Catherine Morland. Her sister might remind you of Isabella Thorpe. The fact that there is a secret relationship might bring to mind thoughts of Frank Churchill and Jane Fairfax. And then, there are the nods to *Persuasion* and *Sense and Sensibility* which I will leave for you to discover.

If you would like to share your observations about which elements you thought were Austen-inspired, you can do that in my *Touches of Austen Readers Group* on Facebook.

Happy Reading!

Chapter 1

Grace Love was not the sort of lady who sat along the wall during dances. She was not the sort of lady who stayed at home when there was an outing to the park. She was not the sort of lady who avoided any sort of fun. Or, at least, she had not been such a lady until now. And all it had taken for Grace's world to change had been one house party.

Through narrowed eyes, she watched the progress of her sister's hat as the carriage Felicity was perched in made its way down the street.

"Grace, dear, do not spill your tea on that chair."

"Of course, Mama." Grace pulled her attention back to the sitting room in the townhouse they were renting for the season and away from her traitorous sister.

"Is it not wonderful that Mr. Ramsey has followed Felicity to Bath?" Mrs. Love had crossed to the window to almost, but not quite, peek out of the window. She stood so that she was concealed by the drapery while she attempted to look down the street.

"Of course, Mama." Grace knew that her mother was hopeful that this match would take for Felicity since the last one had not and the circumstances surrounding the dissolution of that match had not placed Grace's sister in a favourable light.

Therefore, every effort was to be made on Felicity's behalf. One did not cry off an attachment to very many gentlemen before she was marked as a lady to be avoided at all costs.

The tea in Grace's hand had lost its appeal. She forced one last sip of it before discarding her cup to the table next to her chair.

Felicity's reticence to commit to just one gentleman had completely shattered any hope Grace had of a wonderful season, for, to help her sister, Grace had been required to give up half of her new dresses and was to accept only a fraction of the invitations she received. Next year could be hers. Once Felicity was married. Until then, she was relegated to the position of a lesser relation – a toad-eater. Her lips curled in disgust.

She rose from her chair. "I think I shall go up and read."

"You are a good sister." Her mother favoured her with a pleased smile from where she still stood, almost peeking out of the window. "Who knows, if this drive goes well, you may have a season after all."

"Of course, Mama." Grace forced a smile to her lips. How had she thought her sister was all that was good? How did one live her whole life with another person and not realize that the person sharing your maid was horrid?

Filled with morose thoughts and dashed hopes, she trudged up the stairs to her room. She had thought at one time it would be wonderful to be Felicity, for her sister seemed so cunning, so self-assured, so worldly-wise — and it was not as if her sister was not all those things. She was. It was just that she used them to promote herself at the expense of others – including her own sister.

Grace flopped on her bed and stared at the ceiling. She had very little desire to read. She had only used reading as an excuse to avoid the hopeful effusions of her mother, which she knew would follow Felicity's departure and would not cease until Felicity returned and could add to the chatter about her good fortune.

Was Mr. Ramsey not the most handsome man ever? Was she not the most fortunate creature in all the world? Grace rolled her eyes at the imagined declarations of her sister. Of course, Felicity would say all this with a sigh and an affected wistful look.

Her sister was fortunate. She was fortunate not to be forcefully betrothed to the man who had taken her for a drive since he and she had been in the garden alone for some time at the Abernathy's house party. And as far as Mr. Ramsey being handsome was concerned – well, any lady who cared to cast a glance in Mr. Ramsey's direction could decipher he was an Adonis. In fact, it was Grace who had first pointed that fact out to her sister when they had arrived at the house party.

"I said it because I was considering him," she told the orange ball of fluff that curled up at her side. "You know, Philomena, I was also the one to suggest that Mr. Clayton would make a good catch. His living is not small, and he has such a gentle spirit." She sighed as she ran her hand through her cat's fur. "I should not have said a word. I should have kept all my thoughts to myself, for if I had not said anything, perhaps, I would be installed in a parsonage or be driving with Mr. Ramsey now." She huffed. "And I would be riding in Hyde Park, not in Bath, for I would not have put my reputation in danger."

Philomena mewed her agreement, and Grace rewarded her with a scratch behind her ear.

Before the end of the Abernathy's house party, everyone had heard of Felicity's walk to the garden pavilion with Mr. Ramsey and Mr. Carlyle. That bit of interesting and potentially scandalous news had grown in interest once it was discovered that Mr. Clayton had gone home with his hopes dashed. It did not help either when Felicity, who was unaware of the betrothal which had happened in her absence, attempted to begin a rumor about Miss Hamilton's hair ribbon being in Mr. Carlyle's possession after they had spent a few private moments together.

"Grace."

Grace pushed up onto her elbows and looked toward her bedroom door as it opened slowly.

"You are not reading!" her mother cried, coming into the room.

"I could not ignore Philomena," Grace retorted.

"No, I could not do that, could I, sweetling?" she said to her cat, who once again mewed in agreement.

Her mother gave her an appraising look. "Your time will come. There is no need to sulk overly much because your sister must be put forward. Indeed, your time might be sooner than expected." Her eyes lit with excitement.

"I do not see how," Grace grumbled. "What if Felicity decides someone else is better than Mr. Ramsey as she did with Mr. Clayton?"

Mrs. Love pushed Philomena to the side and took a seat on the bed. "Oh, she will not. She cannot be that stupid."

Grace was not sure she agreed. Stupid was giving up a kind gentleman like Mr. Everett Clayton for a handsome gent who carried himself with a trifle too much assurance. One could not possibly be so attractive as Mr. Ramsey and not know it. At the thought, it occurred to Grace that perhaps she should be happier that her sister had been stupid, or she might find herself tied to that very Adonis-like gentleman who thought too well of himself.

No, she scolded herself, that was bitterness talking – although — Mr. Ramsey had been willing to sneak away in the garden with Felicity when everyone knew that Felicity and Mr. Clayton were nearly betrothed, so maybe it was not bitterness but truth?

"Have you heard a word I said?"

Grace blinked and looked at her mother. "No?" Had her mother been speaking?

"I thought not, for I expected you to be far more excited than you are at such wonderful news."

Grace's brow furrowed. "What wonderful news?"

"You received a letter."

"You opened it?" Grace cried when her mother handed her an unfolded letter.

"I am your mother."

"But it was mine." Just like the three new gowns hanging in Felicity's wardrobe were supposed to be in her wardrobe but were not.

"And I have given it to you."

"But you read it first. Now the news is not as special."

"Oh, I think it is."

"It cannot be since I did not know of it first," Grace retorted before turning her eyes to the missive she held.

"The Sheltons are coming to Bath with your cousin, Bea."

"Mama! You should have let me read it!"

"I am letting you read it, but the news is so exciting. They have asked if you could join them at the house they are renting. It is just outside of town, but not far. You know how Bea is about crowds of people. I suspect that is the reason."

Grace's eyebrows rose as she read the invitation. She knew that Mr. Shelton and Miss Hamilton, who was now his wife, liked her despite her "trollop of a sister." She fought to keep her lips from curling in amusement at Mr. Shelton's description of Felicity. However, it still surprised her that she would be asked to join them as a special guest. After all, Mr. Graeme Clayton could not much care for the family of the lady who had injured his brother.

"I wonder if Mr. Everett Clayton will be with them?" Part of her hoped he would be, while the less vengeful, more logical side of her brain hoped he was not. While she would find it quite delightful for Felicity to have to wonder about whether Mr. Clayton was sharing his tale with the other gentlemen in Bath, Grace would also feel dreadful about Mr. Clayton having to see her sister flirting with Mr. Ramsey.

"Oh, I should think not. He is not mentioned, and I truly think he would be if he were coming with them." Her mother shook her head. "He is best off in town, far from here."

"Far from Felicity," Grace muttered.

"I would not say such, but yes," her mother said. "It is better to not be reminded of one's disappointment."

"There is that," Grace agreed.

"And he might harm Felicity's chances. I cannot believe you hid her behavior from me for so long."

Grace closed her eyes. She had been through this with her mother more than once already. "I did what Felicity asked. I will not make the same mistake." Ever. Nor would she lose another gentleman to her sister. Ever.

"I know you will not. You are a good girl." Mrs. Love patted her youngest daughter's leg. "And now you will not have to sit around watching your sister have fun. I am not so blind as you might think. I know you are unhappy, and I cannot blame you. But your time will come."

"Of course, Mama."

"You are a good girl." Her mother patted her leg once more before rising to leave the room. "I will send your maid to help you pack."

"Mama, there are yet two days until they say they will call."

"One cannot be too prepared," her mother said as she left the room.

Yes, one could be. If one's clothing was all in a trunk when she needed to wear some of that clothing, one would most definitely be too prepared. Grace flopped back on the bed and reread her letter.

"I wonder if they would allow you to join me?" she asked Philomena. "I will ask." She sighed and smiled – not just with her lips but with her whole being as she contemplated being in company once again with Miss Hamilton – no, she was Miss Hamilton no longer. She was now Mrs. Shelton.

"It will be delightful," she said with a sigh. "Two married ladies and their husbands, and not a sister in sight to tell me that the eldest should marry first." She giggled softly. "Would it not be a lark indeed if I were to marry before Felicity?"

Philomena mewed her agreement before snuggling in for a sleep while Grace stroked her fur and dreamed of handsome gentlemen who only had her with whom to flirt.

Chapter 2

"I do not see why Grace had to come with us."

Walter Blakesley peeked over his morning paper to see the source of the comment. She was a fair-looking young lady with a pleasing figure and a dignified carriage. Not his sort. Such an air of grandeur was more likely than not accompanied by fits of temper when the chit did not get her way. He turned his attention back to the news from last night's soirees.

"And leave her at home?"

Walter chuckled. The mother sounded shocked, but he reckoned that an opinionated young miss spouting her opinions should not come as a surprise to the young lady's mother. He held his paper in place as if he were reading it but turned his attention to what he was certain was going to be an interesting conversation between mother and daughter as they strolled past where he sat in the Sydney Gardens.

"She has enough gowns for the number of soirees she will be attending. There is no need for her to follow us around from shop to shop."

"I do not believe we are in a shop."

He peeked around his paper so he could match a face with the voice of the young lady, most likely the aforementioned Grace, who had just spoken. His lips curled up with pleasure. Grace had all the beauty of the first young lady with none of the regal air. However, she looked as if she possessed a good dose of pertness.

"We will be," the first young lady retorted. "And then you will be bored and saddened." She wore a forlorn expression. "I am only thinking of your comfort, my dear sister."

"Are you, indeed?" Grace's tone spoke of uncertainty, but the manner in which her lashes fluttered spoke of her being wise to the true intent of her sister.

Walter turned his attention back to the sister. She pursed her lips and shrugged.

"I suppose it will be good preparation for when you have a season next year, but do not blame me if you weary of all that needs to be done long before it is complete."

"Come now, Felicity," the mother cajoled. "You will be happy to have Grace's opinion on how well you look. I know you will. She has very good taste."

Felicity gave Grace an appraising look. "I suppose so," she agreed and then smiled broadly. "I do hope we see Mr. Ramsey today. I told him we were to go shopping when he asked if he might take me for a drive again this afternoon, but with so much to do before we visit the Upper Rooms tomorrow, I assured him it would not be possible."

She leaned toward her mother and lowered her voice so that Walter had to strain to hear her.

"He made me promise him the first set."

"Oh, that is delightful!" her mother cried.

The Upper Rooms. Tomorrow. Walter made a mental note of the detail. He would most certainly like to see who this Mr. Ramsey was, for he seemed an excellent choice from how the mother was going on about him at present. He lowered his paper and folded it. Looking up, he caught Grace watching him.

He smiled and nodded. To his great amusement, she flashed a quick smile and then turned away as if she had not seen a thing, only to glance back at him after they had turned down a path away from where he sat. With any luck, tomorrow's outing to the Upper Rooms would be one of the soirees which Grace would attend.

"What are you about, Blakesley?"

"Just reading my paper and taking in the view, Mr. Norman. Do you have the morning free from patients?"

Mr. Norman was one of the many physicians who made a good living off of the people who came to Bath to take the waters and improve their health.

"I do not need to see anyone for another hour." Mr. Norman took a seat next to Walter. "The view from here is not without its pleasant aspects." He cut a sly look at his friend.

"Indeed, it is not. However, I do not think that the mother of those two is looking for a physician either for herself or her daughters."

Mr. Norman chuckled. "They look a bit young for my liking."

"Still set on finding a spinster?"

Mr. Norman nodded. "As long as she is not older than thirty or younger than twenty-seven. I think a gap in age of at least four years but not more than seven is ideal."

"You have very odd notions," Walter countered. "I dare say that both of those ladies are more than seven years younger than me."

"A gap of more than seven years is perfectly fine for you. It just is not for me."

"I do believe the infirmities of your patients have addled your brain. How can it be one thing for you and another for me?" Walter said as he rose.

"Are you visiting tenants or just taking your ease today?" Mr. Norman asked as he also rose.

"I have a couple of things that need my attention, but then, I am free."

"Good, good. Then you can keep me company for an hour."

"I just said I had things that needed attention."

"Yes," the good doctor said, taking out his watch, "but only a couple, which is not more than two. I am certain you will have time to complete all that needs doing if you start an hour later than now. In fact, it will not even be an hour." He snapped the cover of his watch closed. "I will need to return to my office in half an hour to prepare for my next visit."

"Oh, very well, then. You may accompany me on my way."

"That sounds like an excellent plan. Where are we off to first?"

"To see a man about a jacket."

"Another jacket? Do you not have enough already?" Mr. Norman hurried after Walter.

"This one is more generously proportioned." Several of his jackets were no longer comfortable to wear for anything more than sitting still while having a portrait painted. Not that he had any plans for commissioning portraits of himself – let alone having one done of him in an ill-fitting jacket.

Mr. Norman chuckled. "Did I not tell you that too many Sally Lunns would do that?"

Walter shook his head. "It is not the Sally Lunns. I have taken up pugilism." He made a fist and bent his arm. The fabric over his upper arm strained against the muscles flexing beneath it. "I believe it was you who recommended physical activity once when you were watching me eat a Sally Lunn." His lips curled into a smirk. "By all rights, I should be sending you the bill for the wardrobe improvements your advice has necessitated."

"I did not specifically say you should take up boxing. Dancing and walking would not require new clothing."

"I walk enough as it is. I wish for something more if I am to exercise."

"Fencing is another option."

"It is a great sport. I must agree. However, I have done that for years – even before your recommendation – and before you suggest it, I also ride. Pugilism seemed the one remaining sport of interest that required a great deal of exertion."

"Yes, well, I am not paying for your jackets. Your pockets are far deeper than mine," Mr. Norman said with a laugh.

"Put it on my account, and at the first sign of gout, I will collect what I am owed in service."

Mr. Norman continued laughing. "If I were a surgeon, you'd likely have better luck at collecting the cost of your coats. How many stitches have you had so far?"

"Counting this one," he pointed to a small scar above his left eye, "three. I am not fond of having my head knocked about. I spend most of my time hitting things that cannot hit back. Sacks of grain, saplings, and the like."

"You hit trees?" Mr. Norman cried. "I am surprised your hands are not in worse shape than they are."

"An old rug softens the blow. You do not expect me to put any of the trees in the orchards at risk, now do you?"

"I suppose I do not, but just the same, it must cause some injury."

Walter removed the glove from his right hand. "A bruise or two." He showed his friend the yellowish-green bruise that a tree had inflicted upon him.

"It looks as if it is healing well, but I will still caution you about such things. A body can only survive a beating so many times before it begins to take a toll."

Walter was just putting his glove back on and about to enter his tailor's shop when a carriage came to a stop a few feet from where he stood.

"Your view has followed you," Mr. Norman whispered as the occupants of the carriage began to disembark.

"Why can you not wear the pair of gloves you purchased in London?" the mother asked.

"There is a hole in the right one."

"I am sure it can be fixed," her mother offered.

"But to wear a damaged pair of gloves to a ball, Mama? What will the gentlemen think of me?"

"Do you really think Mr. Ramsey will mind?" Grace asked.

"I will not only be dancing with Mr. Ramsey," Felicity replied. "I cannot. It would be scandalous to dance every set with the same gentleman."

"But is he not the one gentleman whom you wish to have think well of you?" Grace asked as she followed behind her mother and her sister toward the store just two doors down from Walter's tailor.

"Oh, indeed!" Felicity cried. "But to gain his favour, I must not lose the favor of everyone else. Who would wish to marry a lady who was thought too poor to have a fine pair of gloves?"

"Who indeed?" Walter said to Mr. Norman.

"I am sure I cannot say," Grace answered her sister in a tone that spoke of her wishing very much to say something other than what she had said.

"You may wear my old pair. I am certain it will not harm your chances at all."

"That's a pleasant one," Mr. Norman whispered

as he opened the door to the tailor shop. "If only every lady had such a generous sister."

"Your tongue is as sharp as your knife," Walter quipped. Giving one last look toward the shop just two doors down, he caught the eye of Grace, who once again smiled but turned away quickly and looked as if she had seen nothing. It was a very odd thing. Most young women would smile and then duck their heads before peeking at a fellow again – his thought was interrupted as Grace once again turned her eyes towards him and smiled before stepping into the store into which her mother and sister had already disappeared.

"Did you see that?" he asked Mr. Norman.

"See what?"

"The way that young lady keeps secretly smiling at me?"

Mr. Norman peeked down the street. "I cannot say I noticed."

"She did it in the gardens as well."

"Then, I would venture to guess you have an admirer."

"But why is she so secretive?"

Mr. Norman shook his head. "I am certain that even I am not capable of understanding the working of the female brain, especially the young female brain. If I were, I might not be looking for a spinster. Do you know that not one of the ladies whose care I have taken on has a companion that is less than forty? It is rather odd."

Odd seemed to be the word of the day when it came to ladies. Walter took one more look down the street at where Grace had been. He should not think about her. She was an oddity, the sort of lady which a gentleman of proper standing and great responsibility such as himself should avoid. He really should not think about her, but, unfortunately, his insatiable curiosity had already latched onto the pretty riddle named Grace.

Chapter 3

"Beatrice!" Mrs. Love cried when her niece entered the sitting room. "It has been this age since we have seen you."

"Yes, nearly a year," Mr. Love added. "Mr. Clayton," he added with a bow. "It is a pleasure to see you both."

"And it is a pleasure to see you both as well."

Grace was not certain that Mr. Clayton was speaking truthfully. He seemed to be holding himself rather stiffly, and Bea seemed to have a firm grip on his arm. Grace could not blame him. Felicity had treated his brother abominably.

"My sister is still abed," Grace offered to Bea. "She will be sorry to have missed you, but when one spends a great deal of time dancing into the night, one simply cannot be roused too early in the morning. Or so I hear."

Mrs. Love made a small clicking sound that spoke of disapproval nearly as much as the look Grace's father wore did.

"Is it not true?" Grace asked in her most startled voice in an attempt to cover the jibe she had made about her current, lack-of-a-season circumstances.

"Yes, it is true," her mother said.

"Oh! I am glad. I thought for a moment I had misspoken," Grace said with a little laugh. Her mother looked mollified while her father seemed skeptical, but then, he had always been harder to fool than her mother.

"Please, have a seat. Would you care for some tea or perhaps a glass of port?" Mr. Love asked.

"No, we cannot stay long," Beatrice replied as Graeme helped her to take a seat.

He was so attentive. He had even been so before he married Beatrice. Grace had not been unaware of the care he gave her cousin when she had been at Heathcote last year. The hand on Bea's elbow accompanied by the whispered "Are you well?" made Grace wish to sigh, but she refrained and merely smiled at the sight. One day, she would have a gentleman who would be so thoughtful and caring.

"Mr. and Mrs. Shelton are expecting us to return quickly so that we can make plans for today and tomorrow," Bea continued.

"Do you not just love Miss Hamilton — I mean Mrs. Shelton?" Grace asked eagerly.

Bea smiled softly as she often did. There was such a sweet, gentleness about her. Grace had not admired it so very much until now. It was in complete contrast to Felicity.

"She is lovely," Bea assured Grace. "I understand you became friends at a house party?"

Grace nodded eagerly. "We did. Mr. Shelton, Mrs. Shelton, Mrs. Berkley — that is Mr. Shelton's sister — and myself. I have not made such good friends in some time. I truly have missed them, though Mrs. Shelton writes to me regularly." Excitement bubbled up inside her. Soon, very soon, she would be reunited with friends – true friends. And then, she would begin her quest to become friends with Bea instead of just being cousins.

Mr. Clayton chuckled. "Even Shelton seems eager to have you visit. If Mrs. Shelton had been feeling better this morning, they likely would have joined us." He looked at Mrs. Love. "Yesterday's travel fatigued her."

"I am surprised it has not fatigued Bea as well," Mrs. Love cried. "She has always been so delicate."

"She would not have missed seeing you for the world," Mr. Clayton replied.

"Indeed, I would not," Bea agreed.

"Are you certain you do not wish for tea?" Mr. Love offered once again.

"A cup would be welcome," Bea answered. "If it is not too much trouble that is."

"My husband has been wishing for a cup of tea for this past half hour. You do him a great service by accepting his offer. Does she not, my dear?" Mrs. Love said.

"It is quite a noble service you render me, Bea." His lips curled into an amused smile. "I am still allowed to call you Bea even though you are a married lady, am I not?"

Bea laughed. "Of course. Only my last name has changed. You are still my uncle."

Grace's father sobered somewhat. "I had hoped that you would still claim me as such even after all that has passed." His eyes focused on Mr. Clayton, who nodded.

"Yes, well," Mrs. Love said uneasily, "we are hopeful." She shrugged and sighed.

"As are we," Mr. Clayton replied.

Grace longed to ask about Mr. Everett Clayton, but, knowing how that might upset everyone, she did what was prudent instead of what was wished and held her tongue.

"Your drive was good? The weather seemed perfect for it, yesterday," Mr. Love continued the conversation with only a small amount of unease in his voice.

Grace's father had been most displeased to hear about how his eldest daughter had treated Mr. Everett Clayton. Grace was certain he felt the folly of Felicity's actions much more than her mother did, for Mama tended to move on easily from a disappointment with a hopeful optimism about the future while Papa was more prone to ponder and stew.

"It was most pleasant yesterday," Mrs. Love agreed. "Felicity, Grace, and I even took a walk in the Gardens before we visited the shops. Dry paths and roads. Almost no clouds in the sky, and you could just feel spring in the air. It was delightful. Simply delightful."

"Our drive was just as it should be," Bea assured her. "We could not have ordered better weather than what we were given."

She likely would have said the same if it was raining. Bea rarely complained about anything – not even a cousin who connived to steal the attention of a friend from her. Grace sighed.

"Is something amiss," her father asked.

Grace shook her head. "No, I... I was just thinking about Philomena." Her cheeks warmed at the lie. She was doing nothing of the sort. She was regretting how she had helped Felicity charm Mr. Everett Clayton, but she could not say that!

"Who is Philomena?" Mr. Clayton asked.

"My cat."

"Will she be joining us?" he added with a smile.

He was offering to let her cat accompany her?

"I had not thought it proper to ask if she could." Though she had considered asking for some time before deciding it would be too forward to do so.

"I understand Mrs. Shelton was required to leave her cat at home," Mr. Clayton continued. "It might be a welcome surprise if your Philomena is not averse to ladies other than yourself doting on her."

"That cat will not turn down attention," Mr. Love said with a laugh before rubbing his hands together in satisfaction as the tea tray arrived. "Much like I will not refuse a tea cake and a cup of tea."

For the next several minutes, the conversation revolved around pets, sweets, and the weather. The whole event only took twenty minutes according to the clock in the corner, but to Grace who was eager to be off, it seemed a great deal longer. However, as is almost always the case, time did march forward and soon all Grace's things had been tied to Mr. Clayton's carriage, and she and Philomena were seated across from Bea and Mr. Clayton while the vehicle began its journey to the house where Mr. and Mrs. Shelton awaited her arrival.

Grace held the leash she had affixed to Philomena's collar in one hand while stroking her with her other hand. She blew out a breath and pulled in a deep, fresh one.

"I take it you are happy to be away from home." Mr. Clayton said.

"I am happy to be away from Felicity," Grace answered honestly. "I cannot apologize enough for her behaviour. Your poor brother." She looked down at the cat beside her. "Is he well? I have worried about him."

"He will be."

"Is he in town?"

"No."

"He is not in Bath, is he?" Grace asked in surprise.

Mr. Clayton chuckled. "No, he is at home. He will go to town for a time perhaps in a month or so."

"That is too bad."

"I am not sure I see why it is a bad thing that he is at home and not in Bath. Was there a reason you wished he was here?"

Grace's eyes grew wide, and she shook her head as mortification spread like a fire across her cheeks. "I had not intended to say that aloud."

"Ah, but you have, and so now you must explain it."

"Graeme," Bea said softly, "I do not think it is necessary."

"No, no. He is right. I would be tormented with curiosity if I were him," Grace assured her cousin. There was no way she was going to be the cause of an argument between Bea and Mr. Clayton. "It is disgraceful to admit it."

"Then, you do not need to," Mr. Clayton assured her.

Grace shook her head. "You have been very gracious in not breaking with my family over how shabbily my sister treated your brother. I shall admit what I was thinking so that you can know where I stand in relation to the whole horrid affair."

"I think I can tell as it is," Mr. Clayton said. "Mr. Shelton has told me about your disapproval of what your sister did."

Of course, Mr. Shelton did. Best friends did not keep secrets. Her cheeks warmed even further. "Did he tell you that I found your brother attractive when I first arrived at Heathcote?"

Mr. Clayton shook his head.

Hmm. It seemed gentlemen did keep some secrets from their best friends. She would have to remember that. She ran a hand along Philomena's fur.

"Well, I did," she said, "but that is not the disgraceful thing I must admit. While I am happy that Mr. Everett Clayton is not going to have to see my sister and be reminded of her duplicity, I almost wish he were here to tell his tale and ruin my sister's chances in Bath." She looked from one startled face across from her to the other. "I told you it was disgraceful. It is not at all what a lady should wish for her sister, and yet I do."

If it were not for the wheels turning along the road and the clipping and clopping of horse's hooves, the carriage would have been entirely silent for several minutes.

"We are hopeful that she will make a match with Mr. Ramsey, for if she does not, I fear I will never get a season."

"I do not understand," Mr. Clayton said.

"The hope of my sister's success comes at the cost of my season."

"You are not here for the season?" Mr. Clayton asked in surprise.

Grace shook her head. "Not my own season. I was to be allowed to attend a few soirees, but the focus must be my sister, you see."

Across from her, Mr. Clayton smiled broadly.

"I do not see how that is a happy thing," she said.

"He is not happy about your situation," Bea assured her. "He is happy for Mr. Shelton."

Grace's brow furrowed. She had no idea what her lack of a season had to do with Mr. Shelton.

"Shelton imagines himself somewhat of a matchmaker," Mr. Clayton said, "and since you were unsuccessful at the house party, he was hoping for a second chance to prove himself."

How wonderful! Grace clapped her hand in delight!

"I take it you are not distressed by this news?" Bea questioned cautiously.

"Not at all!" Grace assured her. "I shall welcome the adventure."

She settled back against the squabs and sighed. How the state of one's life could change in an instant from dreary to hopeful! It was remarkable. Would it not make Felicity jealous to see her sister on the arm of some handsome beau? Oh, the thought was nearly too delicious to consider without giggling until...

She gasped and shrank into herself a little as the thought struck her. Her sister must not know of any possible matches for if she did... well, that was how she had discovered both Mr. Everett Clayton and Mr. Ramsey.

And, in the blink of an eye, life was back to dreary.

Chapter 4

"I was sorry to have missed you yesterday, Blakesley."

Walter turned away from studying the couples lining up for the first dance and toward the gentleman who had greeted him.

"Mr. Clayton." He gave him a shallow bow. "It was unfortunate that I could not greet you at Erondale, though I suspect it was poor planning on my part. I should have waited another day before calling. However, I was anxious to make sure that all was well and as you expected it should be."

"I understand you had to replace your housekeeper rather suddenly, so I can understand your anxiety about things."

"Apoplexy is not just a scourge of the wealthy. Of course, my friend, Mr. Norman could tell you more about that." Walter motioned to the fellow next to him. "Mr. Clayton, if I may, this is Mr. Norman, one of the many physicians here in Bath, and in my opinion, one of the best. Mr. Norman, Mr. Clayton."

"It is a pleasure to meet you. I had hoped to gain an introduction to a man of medicine from Blakesley. I knew that if anyone knew precisely who I should meet, it would be him." Graeme leaned forward. "I think that was the one thing at which he excelled in most in college – knowing who was who and what was what."

"He does have an ear for such things," Mr. Norman agreed.

"Someone needs to," Walter inserted. "Mr. Clayton's wife has a delicate constitution," he added in a whisper.

Graeme smiled broadly. "More so now than most times, though no one is to know that."

"And you have brought her to Bath in spite of her condition?" Walter asked in surprise.

"She would not have it any other way. Her constitution might be delicate, but her will is not."

Walter chuckled. "I would assume that is a good thing since she is married to you."

Graeme only shrugged and smiled in response.

"I will introduce her to you as soon as I can pry her away from Mr. and Mrs. Shelton and Miss Love."

Walter's eyes roved over the crowd as best they could. "You should come earlier so that you might get seats in the gallery," he said in passing to Mr. Clayton.

"It is rather a crush," Graeme agreed. "I think if my wife had known it would be so, she might have allowed me to persuade her to stay at Stratsbury Park."

"Not a fan of large groups of people, is she?"

"Not normally, but there are inducements to enduring it now, you see."

"Such as?" Mr. Norman inquired.

"She has never had a season and thinks that it is best to experience one before she becomes a mother so that she can be prepared for what her child will experience in seventeen years or so."

Walter chuckled.

"Bea likes to be prepared for all eventualities," Graeme offered.

"Different sides of the same coin, then," Mr. Norman muttered.

"Quite," Graeme agreed.

"It seemed to me that such is also true of Shelton

and his wife." Walter's lips tipped up as he finally found for whom he was looking. Mr. Shelton was bending to hear what a very pretty young lady named Grace was saying. Miss Love was it? "Is that your guest with Mr. Shelton?" he asked Graeme.

"Yes, that is Miss Love. Would you care for an introduction?"

Yes, yes, he would very much like to meet the secretive Miss Love. "If it is not a bother," he replied with an air of indifference before following Graeme across the room.

"How do you know her?" he asked as they moved through the gathered throng.

"She is my wife's cousin."

"Ah, I see. Mr. Shelton said that you were collecting her in Bath, does she have family here?"

"Yes and no. Her mother, father, and sister are here for the season."

"An unmarried sister?" Walter asked as if he did not already know such a thing to be true.

"Yes, and not worth your time." There was a cold bitterness to Graeme's tone that was curious.

"Then, you shall have to point her out to me so that I might avoid her." A thing which he had already intended to do. He had both seen and heard enough from the other Miss Love to inform him that a wide berth around her would be best.

"Gladly," Graeme replied.

There must a story of great interest behind such an emphatic response. Perhaps over time, Walter would discover it, but for now, he was about to meet the mysterious Grace – after he met Mrs. Clayton, that is. Blasted propriety that stood in the way of satiating curiosity!

"Oh!" Grace cried upon being introduced to Walter. "I believe I saw you yesterday in the gardens."

"I believe you are correct. You do look familiar and that must be where I saw you."

"And then you visited a tailor," Grace added. "Felicity – that's my sister – was in need of a new pair of gloves," she explained to the group.

"Did she find what she needed?" Walter asked. This young lady was as delightfully entertaining as her secret smiles had told him she might be.

"Felicity always finds what she wants," Grace said with a flutter of her lashes.

"Even if someone else has it," Roger Shelton muttered, earning a glare from his wife.

"You are not wrong," Grace assured him. "However, I was fortunate enough to claim her old pair." She held out her hands for inspection. "I should not tell you this, but there was the tiniest tear right here." She pointed to a spot just above her left wrist. "But I dare anyone to know that it is there."

"Your needlework is exemplary, Miss Love. I would not have thought that those rosebuds hid a blemish. It is very well done." Walter was not prevaricating. She had done a marvelous job of disguising the tear and making the gloves even more lovely than they originally had been. She was a clever young woman.

"It is, is it not?" she agreed with a pleased smile.

Clever, and not unwilling to claim such a thing.

"Would you allow me the privilege of a dance?" he asked. Her eyes grew wide at the offer and her head shook ever so slightly. She was refusing him?

"I am sorry," she said softly, "but I was hoping for someone else to claim my hand for the next dance." Her cheeks grew rosy.

"No one has asked you," Shelton muttered.

"No, but if I give this dance to Mr. Blakesley then I will not be free if another arrives to ask."

Roger Shelton's brow furrowed. "You did not mention this before."

"Because I did not know the gentleman's name. One must not speak of a hope to dance with someone to whom she has not been introduced." She cast a glance in Mr. Norman's direction. "However, that is no longer a problem."

"Norman?" the question flew out of Walter's mouth.

Grace's head bobbed up and down. "Though it is forward to even admit to it."

Forward was not the word Walter would use for it. "Well, then, Norman, do not keep the lady waiting." Walter knew his tone was less than gracious.

Grace put a hand on his arm but then withdrew it quickly. "Do not be discouraged, Mr. Blakesley. It is not that I do not wish to dance with you. It is just that I had hoped to speak to Mr. Norman."

"You had?" Roger echoed the question in Walter's mind.

"Yes, I would like some advice." Her hands were twisting in a nervous sort of fashion. "About a condition."

What was she about?

"You wish to speak to him because he is a physician?" Mrs. Shelton's tone was incredulous.

Grace's head bobbed up and down as she pulled

her lower lip between her teeth. Walter would put ten pounds on it that the chit was lying.

"You did not know he was a physician until just now," Mrs. Clayton said.

"But he looked like one," Grace declared.

"He looked like one?" Skepticism filled Roger's question. Apparently, no one else quite believed Miss Love's story any more than Walter did.

"And what is your condition?" Mr. Clayton asked, earning him a disapproving "Graeme" from his wife.

"Oh, it is merely a curiosity, really."

"About what?" Graeme pressed.

Grace tapped her chest.

"Your heart?" Walter said. "Are you not a trifle young for such a thing?"

Grace fluttered her lashes at him. "Did I say it was my heart?"

"It seemed as if you did," Roger inserted.

"Well, it might be, or it might not be. If you would all just allow Mr. Norman to ask me to dance, then after I have spoken to him, he can share what he knows with his friend and I will tell you all about it on our ride home." Her brow furrowed. "I am not intentionally being rude to Mr.

Blakesley." She huffed. "Do not look at me as if I am my sister."

The last comment raised several eyebrows, including Walters, for it was spoken with great vehemence.

"Mr. Norman." Walter gave his friend a nudge. "The rest of us are counting on you to discover what we would like to know."

"Miss Love, might I have the pleasure of this dance?" Mr. Norman asked.

"I thought you would never ask." Grace put her hand in his but instead of allowing him to lead her directly to the dance floor, she stopped so that she was standing shoulder to shoulder with Walter, though she was looking toward the dancers and he was looking away. "Please, do not dance with my sister," she whispered and then allowed herself to be swept into the group of dancers.

"That was odd."

"You have never been more correct about anything, Shelton," Graeme agreed.

"What did she say to you just now, Blakesley?" Roger asked.

Walter shook his head in bewilderment. "She

told me not to dance with her sister. I'm beginning to think that Miss Love's sister is akin to poison."

"Very like it," Graeme assured him. He blew out a breath. "She broke my brother's heart," he whispered.

Ah. Things were beginning to fall into place. "My condolences," he muttered.

"It was done in a rather spectacular fashion," Roger added. "You would do well to heed Grace's advice."

Even Shelton was warning him away from the other Miss Love? That added to the weight of caution greatly. Graeme Clayton had never been quite as devil-may-care about things as Roger Shelton had been. Therefore, a warning from Graeme was to be heeded, but, when it was paired with rousing support from Roger, the danger of ignoring such advice would be foolish in the extreme, and Walter was no fool.

"Then, I shall take myself to the card room and await Mr. Norman there."

"You are not dancing?" Mrs. Shelton asked in surprise.

Walter smirked. "It seems the safest way to avoid Miss Love's sister, and I have already suffered rejection once. I am not entirely certain I can survive it a second time, although perhaps if I were to ask a young lady while Norman is occupied and not at my side." He chuckled and shook his head.

If not for the way Miss Love had used a begging sort of tone when she had whispered *please* to him just now, he might have truly felt her rejection far more than he presently did. The word was as tantalizing as her secret smiles, which she flashed at him once again when he looked her direction as she lined up across from Norman. The taunting tease of a woman!

"If you find you change your mind," Mrs. Shelton said, "I am not opposed to dancing and, as much as my husband would rather that I dance every set with him, it is not how things are done. I would not refuse your offer."

"I shall keep that in mind," Walter said with a nod of his head before making his way out of the room to find a table at which to sit and watch others play cards while he and a glass of port contemplated the secrets held by the lovely Miss Grace Love.

Chapter 5

"I saw you dancing."

Grace pasted a smile on her lips. She had been doing her best to not meet up with her mother, for doing so would inevitably lead to having to speak with her sister. And, she was not wrong, for Felicity was at her mother's side, looking all eagerness.

"He was very nice looking and exceptionally light on his feet," Mrs. Love continued.

"Oh, indeed!" Felicity cried. "He might be one of the best dancers here."

"Even better than Mr. Ramsey?" Grace asked. Her sister should be thinking only of Mr. Ramsey, but, of course, she was not.

"Yes, I do believe so, though I would not for all the world tell him so," her sister replied.

"What was his name?" her mother asked eagerly.

"Mr. Norman," Grace replied. "He is a physician."

Her mother gasped and blinked. "A physician? He has no estate?"

A wicked thought captured Grace's imagination. "None of which I know, but he has a home here in Bath. Some rooms somewhere. I really do not know where." Nor did she really know in what sort of accommodation Mr. Norman lived, but rooms had seemed like they would be the most revolting residence. "There is still so much to learn about Bath."

"Rooms?" Felicity repeated. "Not even a townhouse?"

Yes, it was fun to see them both so aghast at her choice of a dance partner. She was certain Felicity would not even attempt to steal Mr. Norman away from her — not even if he was light on his feet, which he was.

"He does not have one yet," Grace quite possibly lied, making a mental note to discuss this with Mr. Norman at some point, "but once he is better established, I am certain he will have a townhouse." If he did not already have one that is. "He seems very intelligent. I have every faith in his ability to become quite successful in his career." She should also likely find out how successful he was at present. They had spoken a little about themselves while dancing, but long drawn out discussions were not meant for the dance floor. Therefore, the focus of their conversation had been about Felicity and Mr. Blakesley.

"Yes, yes. I am sure he will be," her mother muttered.

Grace straightened her glove as she allowed her less than commendable thought from earlier to make itself fully known. "I have given him leave to call on me tomorrow."

"You have not!" her mother cried. "A physician? Grace!"

Grace batted her lashes and looked at her mother in feigned surprise. "Is there something wrong with that?"

"Of course, there is," Felicity snapped. "One does not participate in a season to secure a physician as a husband. One strives for a higher connection."

Grace smiled at her sister. "But I am not here for the season. You are. I am only here because there was nowhere else to send me."

"That is not true." Her mother's whisper was harsh. "We had hoped you would get a partial season and find some success."

"Is that true, Felicity?" Grace asked in as sweet a confused tone as she could.

Her sister looked at their mother in surprise before turning her attention back to her sister. "Of course, it is."

"Then, you will not fault me for wishing to have some success in getting to know Mr. Norman? He is excessively handsome, and from what I hear, he comes from a wealthy family. He was just not born first or even second or third. Sadly, he was fourth, which was a grave oversight on his part. However, he seems quite happy in his chosen occupation, and, from the greetings he received from several people, I would venture a guess that he is well-respected." She looked over her shoulder and then leaned toward her sister and mother as she lowered her voice. "I believe Mr. Clayton will keep him in mind for Bea if there should be a need. I am not certain how she will tolerate Bath. She is not used to so many people, you know."

Mrs. Love looked startled by that revelation. "Is she unwell?"

"No," Grace assured her with all haste. "It is just a precaution. You know how Bea can be. Frankly, I think it is sweet how well Mr. Clayton cares for her." She sighed. "I would not have to worry about good care if I were to decide on Mr. Norman. I do think he would see to the well-being of his wife quite well. You can see his caring nature in his eyes. They are a lovely shade of brown."

She had no intention of ever becoming Mrs. Norman, no matter how kind and compassionate she truly found Mr. Norman. However, neither her sister nor her mother needed to know that.

"Do be serious," Felicity scolded. "He would not have the means to see you set up as you would desire. How many fine dresses could a lady expect to have on a physician's income?"

"Oh, at least, as many as I have now," Grace assured her but then sighed. "Of course, I do not have many at present."

Mrs. Love grasped Grace's hand. "You are a very good sister to give up so much on our sister's behalf. Is she not, Felicity?"

"Yes, very good," Felicity replied.

It would have been a more convincing agreement if Felicity had looked even a smidgeon guilty for what her sister was giving up because of her.

"Oh!" Felicity cried. "I have worn this dress three times now to various functions. I am certain I cannot be seen in it again. So, I will send it to you. With a few alterations, it will be very flattering on you." She ran the ribbon at the waist of her dress between her fingers. "I would change out the embellishments if I were you. That would make it look less like my dress and more as if it has always been yours."

"That is a very generous thing!" Their mother cried. "I will send some lace and ribbon with it."

Right. How very generous. Grace thought ruefully. That dress was supposed to have been hers before it was snatched away for her sister's use.

"However," her mother added in a whisper, "I would caution you against settling on the first gentleman who asks you to dance."

Grace laughed lightly. "Really, Mama. I must find someone to refuse before I can find someone to wed. Mr. Norman seems the perfect sort of gentleman to sustain such a blow. Would you not agree, Felicity? I am certain just by being seen with him, I will become much more sought after."

Their mother scowled. "One does not select gentlemen for the sole purpose of refusing them or increasing one's appeal to others."

Grace blinked. "Oh, I thought we did." She fluttered her lashes at Felicity, who scowled.

"I did not select Mr. Everett Clayton for such a reason," Felicity whispered. "I am certain I would have been quite happy to be Mrs. Everett Clayton had I not met my dear Mr. Ramsey."

"Hmmm." Grace pretended to consider her sister's words. "Then, I suppose, I shall have to spend the rest of the night considering if I would be happy to be Mrs. Norman since I have given the gentleman permission to call on me."

"Truly, Grace," Felicity scoffed, "you are such a simpleton. Have you not learned anything from school or me about securing a good match?"

"Apparently, not. Though I thought I had." She felt the smile she wore down to her toes. Pretending to be interested in Mr. Norman and provoking her sister was delightfully amusing.

~*~*~

"Why did your mother caution me about allowing Mr. Norman to call on you?" Graeme asked as he settled into the carriage later that night.

"Is Mr. Norman calling on you?" Mr. Shelton asked in surprise from the bench across from where Grace sat next to Bea.

"He most certainly is if he can find the time in his schedule," Grace replied. "It is only polite to do so, you know. He did dance with me after all."

"Because you asked him to," Roger returned.

"No, I only said I hoped he would ask me. I did not ask him. The two are very different things."

"I am not certain my sister would agree," Roger said.

Grace could hear the scowl in his words. Her plans had not included angering her friends.

"It was necessary," she said softly. "Your sister is all that is good. Mine is quite the opposite."

"I will not argue that," Roger assured her in a more friendly tone.

"Why just imagine if Felicity thought I found Mr. Blakesley attractive. I just know she would try to snatch him away since that is what she did with Mr. Everett Clayton and Mr. Ramsey."

"Mr. Ramsey, too?" Bea asked in surprise.

Grace nodded. "But Felicity will not bother attempting to snatch away a gentleman who is a physician, even if he has lovely brown eyes and can dance better than anyone I have met. He would be too far beneath her notice." She smiled, still rather amused with herself.

"She also thinks such a gentleman should be beneath my notice." She looked around Bea to Graeme. "As does my mother, which is why she has cautioned you. However, you need not worry. I have no intention of entertaining the idea of becoming Mrs. Norman, and Mr. Norman knows he is only calling on me as a ruse. Everything is perfectly well."

She leaned back against the squabs before popping forward again. "Oh, I forgot to tell you. Felicity is sending me a dress and my mother is including some lace and ribbon. It is the dress she was wearing tonight. The very one which was originally ordered for me before Mama decided we must put all our efforts toward Felicity's happy future."

Victoria Shelton laughed softly. "She is sending you *your* dress?"

"Yes. She has worn it three times and simply cannot be seen in it again." Grace sighed. Sadness washed over her. "Dresses, gentlemen, it seems it is all the same to my sister. What I am supposed to have or what I like must be hers. She really is a self-ish creature. I only wish I had come to that realization sooner."

"Just because she is selfish now, does not mean she will always be so." Bea's voice was soft and soothing.

"Perhaps," Grace agreed. "I cannot believe I spent so many years trying to be just like her. Oh! The unpleasantness of which I have been an unwitting part! It is most shameful to consider. We were not at all nice to you, Bea. I am most grievously sorry for my part in that. Mr. Everett Clayton would have done better—"

"No, he would not have," Graeme interrupted forcefully. "My brother is an idiot. He always has been. While the fault in his unhappiness rests in a large part on your sister's behaviour, he is not blameless. He was led astray by a pretty face and a lively spirit, but he did not go unwillingly. And, while I harbour some ill-feelings toward your sister for the way in which she treated him at the house party, I am not sorry Everett is a daft fool, for it did result in my finding the most perfect bride." He lifted Bea's hand and kissed it.

Grace sighed. "I hope one day to be as happy as you all are."

"You will be," Roger assured her. "I shall see to it."

He was a good friend!

"While you are seeing to it," she said after thanking Roger for his concern, "could you do so in such a fashion that my sister will not know?"

"I am not certain how that is possible," Roger replied.

"We could have a dinner party," Graeme cried. "Your sister would not be at a dinner party, for I would not invite her."

Across from her, Roger nodded his head. "That is an excellent idea."

"Just a small one," Bea begged.

"Yes, yes, nothing too large, my love," Graeme assured her.

"And if I am seen with several gentlemen and not just one in particular –"

"Your sister would think you were not serious about any of them," Roger concluded Grace's thought.

"But what do we do if one gentleman, in particular, catches Grace's fancy and wishes to court her?"

Victoria asked. "Will he not be put out by all the other swains buzzing about his prize? How is that any different from what Miss Love was doing at the Abernathy's house party?"

"That is simple," Roger answered. "By then, the said gentleman will be so far under Grace's spell that not even her trollop of a sister could pry him away from her." He shrugged. "Besides, maybe by then Ramsey will have gained Miss Love's promise or forced her hand."

No, Grace thought as Mr. and Mrs. Shelton continued to argue over whether it was polite to say such a thing about Mr. Ramsey's intentions, *the difference was that the gentleman she fancied would never be amongst the hopeful swains.* At least, he would not be if Mr. Norman played his part well.

Chapter 6

This was foolish.

Walter glanced toward Erondale and then looked at his watch before tucking it back into the pocket of his waistcoat. It was five minutes past the time Mr. Norman had said to be exactly where Walter was. If he was not such a curious sort of fellow, he would have told his friend that there was no way he was taking part in a scheme to meet a lady in such a clandestine fashion. Curiosity he had in great quantity. Patience was in shorter supply in normal circumstances and in extreme want when his curiosity had been excited.

He punched the rug which was wrapped around the tree next to him. If he was to be left standing like a fool in an orchard, he might as well get some benefit from it even if a cravat and waistcoat were not a usual part of his exercise costume. He sighed and hit the tree again before bobbing to the side as if the tree had thrown a punch in return.

Blowing out a breath, he gave Erondale one last glance before turning his focus to punishing the rug and tree and attempting to ignore the prick of impatience which taunted him to satiate his curiosity without waiting a moment longer.

For three jabs and just as many bobs to the side, Walter ignored the pleas of impatience. However, its demands could not be pushed to the side for longer than that. Therefore, after just three punches to the tree, he stopped and donned his jacket.

This was foolishness. He had waited at the spot as required for a quarter of an hour now, and Grace had not met him here as she said she would.

He was going to Erondale. It was his property after all, and those within its walls were his tenants. There was nothing to keep him from calling on them, and it was not as if it was an exceptionally warm day. The breeze had a bitterness to it despite the sky being nearly free from clouds, and he could not just wait under a tree forever.

With his jacket buttoned, straightened, and made as presentable as could possibly be done without the use of a mirror, he put on his greatcoat and hat before untying the rug from the tree and storing it in his gig as he normally did – folded and tucked in the boot.

A quarter of an hour and two days was a long enough wait to find out who the mysterious Grace Love was. Her secret smile had taunted and tantalized him since he first saw it in the park. He would be put off no longer. And so, he urged his horse to traverse the short distance between orchard and house as swiftly as possible.

"Why are you here?" Mr. Norman whispered to Walter when Walter took a seat next to him in the sitting room at Erondale.

"You were late."

"It could not be helped," Norman returned.

"So could not my arrival here." He turned a smile on his hosts who were looking at the two gentlemen curiously. "I beg your indulgence of my poor manners. My friend is somewhat startled to see me as I was supposed to have been engaged elsewhere. However, plans change."

"I hope it was not anything unpleasant which caused your change in plans." Grace was looking at him with concern.

"A prodigious lack of patience," Mr. Norman muttered.

Walter chuckled. "My friend is correct. I seem to be incapable of waiting very long for anything." He looked pointedly at Grace. "Especially if the longed-for item is of great intrigue."

"Oh!" she said with a small gasp and then a smile. "I could not agree more, Mr. Blakesley. I, myself, am frightfully impatient at times when I am anxious for something to happen or a journey to start."

"Miss Grace and I were about to take a drive." Norman lifted an eyebrow as he gave Walter a look of pure displeasure.

If Grace were a spinster, Walter might have been concerned by such a glare. However, he knew that Miss Grace was far too young to meet his friend's requirements for a lady. He also knew that his friend was only playing a part and the lovely lady who was supposed to take a drive with Norman was not actually interested in Norman at all but was rather intrigued by Walter, himself. Such knowledge gave him a great deal more confidence today than he had had last night when Grace had refused him in preference for his friend.

"Well, do not let me keep you from it." Walter waved his hand toward the door.

"We cannot leave now!" Grace cried.

"And why is that?" Mr. Shelton, who was settled very cozily on a settee next to his wife, was smirking at Walter.

If anyone was to figure out that a game was afoot first, it would be a master of games such as Shelton. Of course, he might just be enjoying the prospect of two gents having a tiff over a pretty lady.

"A guest has just arrived, of course," Grace replied.

"But will not Mr. Norman feel..." Shelton furrowed his brow, "how shall I say this? Put out? Perhaps that is it. Will not Mr. Norman feel put out to be made to wait to take you on a drive?"

Grace's mouth popped open but then closed just as quickly, and for the first time since Walter had seen her in the park two days ago, the lady looked befuddled. She had been frustrated and annoyed at the Assembly Rooms when questioned about her desire to dance with Mr. Norman, but she had not looked perplexed as she did now.

She turned wide eyes to Norman. "Will you?"

Norman sighed and shook his head. "Not overly much."

"Mr. Norman likes to keep to a schedule, you see," Walter added.

Grace's head bobbed up and down, though her puzzled expression had not left her face. "But I should not like to be the cause of disappointment."

Walter believed every word of that for she looked rather grieved at the thought.

"I truly did not think you would be put out at all," she added as she reached down to pick up the orange ball of fur at her feet. "I am not very good at this," she muttered as she stroked the cat she now held.

Between her look of sorrow and Norman's look of concern, Walter was beginning to curse his impatience.

"Would you like to walk in the garden instead?" Mrs. Clayton asked. "It is not a drive, but it is a change of place."

Norman shook his head. "I am well. Thank you."

"Are you certain?" Grace asked.

"Yes, I am just sorry –" He did not finish his sentence but shifted his eyes from her to Walter.

Grace sighed. "This is foolish, and precisely why

these sorts of things should not be attempted. Is that not right, Philomena?" The cat meowed at her mistress as if it had understood the question.

"Perhaps you could explain what is foolish." Mr. Clayton was looking for all the world like a displeased and suspicious father or older brother. If it were not for the fact that he was part of the reason for that particular expression on his friend's face, Walter might have chuckled at seeing someone of Graeme's reputation – at least, what it was in college – looking as he did.

"I can explain part," Walter offered.

Graeme's eyes narrowed as he turned them towards Walter.

"At her request, given to me by Mr. Norman, I was to meet Miss Grace in the orchard three-quarters of an hour ago," he snapped his watch closed.

Graeme had now crossed his arms and was looking at Grace with raised brows.

"I only wished to meet him without anyone knowing." Grace leaned forward and whispered, "He is very handsome," to Graeme, which caused Roger to chuckle and Graeme's brow to furrow while Walter could only smile. It was not so dreadful a thing to be called handsome by an intriguing lady like Grace.

"Why could you not meet him here?" Mrs. Shelton asked, and then closed her eyes and shook her head.

"Are you well?" Roger sat forward and looked at his wife.

She shook her head once again and, rising quickly left the room in great haste, followed by her husband.

"Oh, goodness!" Grace cried. "Have I caused her to be ill?"

Mr. Norman shook his head. "It is not you."

"How do you know?" Grace demanded.

"I am a physician and privy to details others might not know."

"What do you mean?" Grace asked.

"I cannot say. I just know that you are not the cause of her illness."

Walter nodded and settled back in his chair. "A bit of tea and toast might help."

"How do you know that?" Grace cried. "You are not a physician."

Graeme shook his head and chuckled.

"Blakesley has an annoying habit of knowing more than he should."

"I am very confused," Grace said. And she looked it.

For all her alluring and secretive actions, Miss Grace Love appeared to be an innocent.

"While we wait for Roger and Victoria to return," Mrs. Clayton said, "perhaps we can hear Grace's reason for arranging a secret meeting with Mr. Blakesley?"

Grace's cheeks flushed very prettily as she ducked her head. "I wished to see if he might wish to be..." she peeked at him, "my secret beau."

"Explain," Graeme demanded.

"I had hoped that we might get to know one another without anyone, most especially my sister, knowing."

"Why?" Walter asked.

"She is horrid," Norman answered for Grace. "That is what I was told," he added, holding up his hands in defense against Walter's shocked expression.

Grace nodded in agreement. "She will attempt to steal you from me. She has done it twice in the last year."

Walter tipped his head and studied Grace. Her hands were busy stroking her cat, but her eyes spoke of the truth of her fear. "Twice, you say?"

She nodded.

Apparently, it was not just gloves and gowns that Miss Love dangled over her sister then.

"Why me?"

Grace shrugged. "You returned my smile in the park."

A returned smile? That was her reason for selecting him? That seemed a rather foolish way to select a suitor.

She ducked her head again. "And you are hand-some."

Well, that did make some sense, he supposed. "You know nothing about me. I could be an adventurer who would only toy with your heart."

Her eyes grew wide. "Are you?"

"No," Graeme answered. "At least, he was not when I knew him in college."

Grace smiled. "I thought from speaking with Mr. Norman that you could not be a scoundrel, for Mr. Norman does not seem the sort to keep company with such people."

"I agreed to meet with you in secret," he cautioned.

"Yes, I have not forgotten that," Graeme grumbled.

"You would not do me harm with Mr. Norman at my side," Grace protested.

"Norman could be a murderer cleverly disguised as a physician. Who would suspect him of such gruesome acts when he is pledged to heal and not harm?" Walter was not sure why he was taking so much pleasure in attempting to dissuade Grace from thinking of him as an upstanding individual who posed little risk to a beautiful young woman. He was, of course, honorable, but she could not have known that from a smile in a garden.

"You are not, are you?" she asked Mr. Norman.

"Would he tell you if he was?" Walter countered.

She looked positively ill as she shook her head. He should stop.

"He is not. At least, as far as I know, he is not, and he has had ample opportunities to do me harm and as you can see, I am well."

Her hand was resting on her heart. "But you are not a lady," she whispered.

"Oh, for the love of all that is good!" Mr. Norman cried. "I am not a murderer! If I were, I would be far more likely to harm Blakesley than anyone else after being treated as I have been today."

Walter laughed. "I apologize, Norman. You are the least likely to do harm to another. Other than to make them drink some horrid concoction designed to improve their health."

"But that is just the sort of person who would be a murderer in a novel," Grace whispered. Her hand was still on her heart, and she was still looking a trifle ill.

"We do not live in a novel," he assured her.

"But do you not think that the ideas found in a novel might have their roots in reality?" she asked in all seriousness.

"In some cases, yes. But not in this one. Mr. Norman is not capable of harming anyone without great provocation. I assure you this is not the first time I have taunted him beyond what is either polite or reasonable, and the worst he does to me is badger me not to eat too many buns and to take some air for my health."

"You are certain?"

"Yes!" Norman cried after giving an exasperated huff.

"The point remains, however," Walter said, "that he could have been, and you could have made an agreement with death. At the risk of sounding far too much like a stern old man, it is an ill-advised thing to be too secretive when you have only just met someone." He smiled at her look of contrition. "That does not mean, however, that we cannot be somewhat secretive in how I call on you."

Her eyes grew wide as a smile spread across her face. "Do you really wish to?"

He sighed. If she kept looking at him as she was, he'd do just about anything for her. Heavens but she was bewitching! "I do, for I am a very curious person, and you, my dear, fascinate me."

Chapter 7

"No, do not turn your head," Mr. Blakesley scolded as he once again sat in the drawing room at Erondale two days later — this time without Mr. Norman and with a screen and drawing paper in front of him.

"But I wish to see what you are doing," Grace replied.

"I am taking your likeness, and I am not very accomplished. Therefore, I beg of you, stay still, or I shall not be responsible for your face looking more like an apple that has been trampled by a herd of pigs than the pretty shape that it is."

"Are you truly so bad?" Grace peeked around the screen.

Truth be told, she did not care what the drawing on the paper looked like. She was far more interested in seeing his face while he sketched, and if that screen was not in the way, she could also see how his mouth moved and eyes narrowed as he shifted his head while studying her. The thought of a gentleman such as Mr. Blakesley studying her likeness so intently was both unsettling in a nervous sort of fashion and exhilarating in a rapid heartbeat that made one smile and sigh sort of fashion.

"You have ruined it." Mr. Blakesley favoured her with a scowl. She was certain she had never met a gentleman who looked so dashing when he scowled.

"It does not look ruined at all," Grace said. Of course, it could be a squiggly mess of knotted lines, and she would think it lovely merely because he had done it. "I shall just put my head back where it was."

She turned and sat as she had been. Or where she thought she had been.

"That is not precisely where you were."

Grace jumped when he poked the back of her head, but thankfully, she did not squeal in fright. That would have been most embarrassing. As it was, Mr. Shelton, who had been designated the chaperone while his wife was resting, was finding the whole process excessively amusing. He rose from his seat and came to where Mr. Blakesley was.

"It will work far better if you were to move her head with both your hands while I study the grid and guide you," he said. "Pushing her head with one hand while trying to keep an eye on these lines will only make things worse."

Grace sucked in a breath as she waited for Mr. Blakesley to place one hand on each side of her head and guide it into position. She might have to peek around the screen again if this were to be the result. She had wondered what his hands must feel like, and until just now, she had not yet been able to discover the answer.

She sucked in a second breath when that for which she had been waiting finally took place, and he actually held her head between his hands. His grip was firm and sure, much as she suspected. A gentleman who practiced boxing trees had to have hands which were as strong as the rest of his person. That is what she had thought, and that was what appeared to be true. If only he could just hold her head and Mr. Shelton could sketch her likeness.

"Now, stay still," he whispered next to her ear

when Mr. Shelton had, at last, said she was in position.

"I am not excessively patient," she replied.

"Do not look at me when you talk." He once again straightened her head.

"I will do my best, but I do like seeing to whom I am speaking."

"Especially when he is so handsome," Mr. Shelton teased.

Grace smiled as Mr. Blakesley muttered a less than polite rejoinder to Mr. Shelton. But, it was true. It was far more interesting to look at a handsome gentleman than a not so handsome one.

Mr. Shelton looked out the window toward the drive. "I will return," he said.

"Is someone here?" Grace asked. Hopefully, it was not her father or her mother coming to call on her.

"Mr. Norman," Mr. Shelton said as he exited the room.

"Why do you suppose Mr. Norman is here?"

"Keep your head still," Mr. Blakesley growled.

"I apologize. It is just such a habit to turn my head when speaking. Do you wish to stop? I do not mind if you do."

He peeked around the screen at her and smiled. "No, I wish to have a likeness of you to put in a frame in my sitting room so that when I have callers and they ask me who that is, I can say it is the image of a mysterious angel whose name is known only to me."

Oh! That was lovely. Grace sighed. Being a mysterious angel was quite a wonderful thing to be.

"And then, they shall beg me to reveal that name, but I shall deny them."

"Would you?"

He nodded. "However, if you cannot remain still, I will not have the chance to refuse to tell them your name."

"Are you teasing me so that you might scold me into sitting still?" That would not be a nice thing to do at all.

He shrugged. "Not entirely."

He ducked back behind the screen, taking away Grace's lovely view and returning her to looking at the empty chair in the corner.

"I do think it would be delightful to have something with which to taunt people. Such a thing likely reflects poorly on my character, but truth be told, I have few who visit me for a social call."

"Do you not have friends?" How did one not have many callers? When she was home, their sitting room was in use constantly for visits from this or that neighbour.

"I have several friends, but I find most of my callers visit me regarding business matters, or to play a game of billiards or drink a bit of port. And none of that happens in my sitting room."

"But a game of billiards is still a social call," Grace protested.

"I suppose it is," he agreed.

"Where do you drink port with your friends?"

"The same place I do business," he replied, "in my study."

"Well, then, that is just where you should place my likeness." She nearly turned her head to smile at him through the screen which would have been stupid since there was no way for him to see anything more than a shadow through the screen.

"That is an excellent idea," he agreed. "I have just your neck left, and I must say it is as lovely a neck as I have ever seen – neither too long, nor too short, and not at all too wide. Quite refined."

A refined neck? Grace stroked down her throat. It did not feel refined. It just felt normal to her.

If she were to be honest, she had never thought a great deal about the appearance of one neck compared to another. She stroked her fingers down her neck again.

"That is very distracting." Mr. Blakesley's voice sounded a bit strained.

"You mean this?" She brushed her fingers down the length of her neck for a third time.

"Yes." He peeked around the screen at her. His eyes swept from her eyes to her neck and then upward to her mouth. "I am almost done," he assured her. "Your lips are as lovely as your neck," he said with a wink before ducking behind the screen once again.

"Should I worry about you attempting to seduce me, Mr. Blakesley?"

His head popped back around to look at her. "No. Not even if I should wish to. I am not that sort of fellow."

"That is good to know." Or, at least, she imagined it was a good thing. "Do you want to?"

"I am quite certain that is not a proper thing to ask," came the response from behind the screen.

"Of that, I am fully aware," Grace assured him. "And, though you cannot see them, I assure you my cheeks are burning at having done so. However, I was merely curious if you were refusing to seduce me only because your character is upstanding or if you were refusing because you do not find me...um..." She was not quite certain how to word what she wanted to say without being even more improper than she had already been.

"You are beautiful," he replied. "I am refusing just because seducing a young lady such as yourself would be wrong, not because you are not tempting."

"Then you are not rakish at all?"

"Not at all."

"Have you ever been?"

Mr. Blakesley chuckled. "Never. Believe it or not, I have never even called on anyone as a possible suitor before."

Grace's brow furrowed and her mouth opened but then closed without making a sound. He had never called on a lady as a suitor before? A gentleman as handsome as he? "Are you teasing?"

"No." He moved his chair so he could see her. "I am done." He held up his handiwork. "It is not as good as it could be, but then, it is my first attempt at doing this since I was a boy and forced to do it for my sisters."

"Truly?"

He nodded.

"I see I have confused you."

"Indeed, you have," she admitted. "Surely, you must be popular at all the balls. Who would not wish to dance with you?"

"Oh, I dance. I am never in want of a partner, and I do make the required calls afterward as is polite and all that. However, I have never singled out one lady on whom to call and become better acquainted."

The door to the drawing room opened, allowing Mr. Shelton and Mr. Norman to enter.

"You look perplexed," Mr. Shelton said to Grace.

She was. "How old are you, Mr. Blakesley?"

"Twenty-seven, nearly twenty-eight, much like Shelton."

Her eyes shifted to Mr. Shelton. "Did you attend college together?"

Mr. Shelton nodded. "We did not always circulate together, but we were well-acquainted and good friends. Blakesley was more apt to be found studying than either Clayton or I were."

"I had a fortune to amass," Mr. Blakesley explained. "Erondale is not a large property, and the estate in Surrey will go to my brother."

"Surrey?" He was not from here?

"Yes, that is where I grew up. This was my mother's father's home."

"And you are here in Bath because of Erondale?"

He nodded. "Mostly. It also seemed a good place to establish myself in property investments since it is a place where people are often looking for accommodations, and I prefer it to London." He smiled and shrugged when her mouth popped open. "There are far fewer orchards in London, which would make my study of pugilism a trifle more challenging."

Well, that did make sense, and Grace had to admit that Bath and Erondale were both beautiful.

"We have sat long enough," he said, rising. "Would you accompany me on a stroll around the garden before I take my leave? If that is acceptable to Mr. Shelton, that is."

"May I?" Grace asked eagerly. She was in no

hurry to have Mr. Blakesley leave. He was not only handsome. He was also interesting.

"Mr. Norman, do you care for a turn of the garden?" Mr. Shelton asked.

Mr. Norman shook his head. "No, I believe I shall wait to speak with Mr. and Mrs. Clayton."

Mr. Shelton leaned back in his chair. "I think I shall wait for Victoria to join me." He chuckled. "Do not look so forlorn, Miss Grace. I shall not keep you from your walk. You may go without me."

Chapter 8

"Which path shall we take today? There were a few flowers emerging from the soil in the side garden last week when I was here. Have you made an inspection of the beds there today?" Walter asked as he and Grace stepped out the garden door. They had made a short circuit of the garden each day when he had called – even yesterday when the clouds were heavy and a mist hung close.

"There are crocuses about to set their blooms."

"Then you have inspected the side garden today?"

Grace nodded. "This morning before breakfast." She pulled in a breath and released it. It was a sound filled with contentment. Grace seemed to enjoy nature as much as he did.

"Gardens are wonderful are they not?" she asked.

"I could not agree more. About the side garden..." He watched as worry etched its way across her face, causing her to pull in her bottom lip and creating a furrow between her eyes. "It is too visible from the drive." He was certain that was what she was thinking, and he was proven right when her head bobbed up and down.

"I wish I could show you the blossoms I have seen, but if my mother should come to call." She shrugged. "One cannot have a secret beau if everyone knows about him."

"This is true," he agreed with a smile. "Then, the back garden it is, and this time we will pass through the gate and take one of the paths beyond the hedge."

Her face lit with excitement. In the short time he had known her, Walter had found that it was never terribly difficult to discover what Grace was feeling as her features were often painted with whatever emotion grasped her in a particular moment. He had seen her playful secret smile, her frustration in attempting to hide her intentions, and her delight, such as was displayed now, when a scheme met with her satisfaction. Those were but a few of her charming expressions.

However, her most beguiling look, which would likely haunt him from today forward, was the look of longing she had worn when he had poked his head around the screen in the sitting room. It had matched his own feeling in that moment, though he sincerely doubted that she knew such a feeling had been on display to him, for she did not seem to be aware of those sorts of things — not that she did not have an understanding or knowledge of them. He suspected she had a general idea, as evidenced by her questions about whether he was rakish or not, but beyond that, he imagined she was relatively innocent. She was not the kind of lady to toy with a gentleman and lead him down a merry path. Where she led, she wished to travel with him, and he was feeling surprisingly content to follow.

"You are very quiet," she said, interrupting his thoughts.

"My apologies, Miss Love."

"Could you call me either Grace or Miss Grace? I find that Miss Love reminds me too much of my sister."

"Very well, I shall call you Grace when we are alone as we are now and Miss Grace when we are in company. Will that satisfy?" It would be no trial for him, for he had been thinking of her as Grace since first setting eyes on her in the garden almost a week ago.

"That would be wonderful." Her whole being seemed to relax into a place of great comfort, the peacefulness of which, in turn, spilled over onto him.

"And will you insist upon calling me Mr. Blakesley or will you favor me with Blakesley or Walter?"

They took three silent steps before she made her reply. "Is there one you prefer above another?"

"No, I cannot say that there is," Walter answered, "I shall leave the selection up to you."

"That is most unusual, is it not?"

He held the gate open for her. "I am not certain I understand the question."

"Does not everyone have a preferred name they wish to be called?"

He shook his head. "Not everyone. For I do not." He secured the gate behind her. "Or perhaps I do, but since I have never played the part of a suitor before, I do not know what it is that I should like a pretty lady, such as yourself, to call me. However, I must say I do enjoy hearing you say Mr. Blakesley."

In truth, his name had never sounded so sweet as it did falling from her lips, which were currently tipped up in a small becoming smile that danced in her eyes.

"That seems sensible. Therefore, I shall try them both, and we shall, together, see which seems best."

He extended his arm to her again. "I think that is a marvelous plan."

"You truly have never courted any other lady?"

He shook his head. "Never."

"Did you wish to?"

Again, he shook his head. "Not particularly. Most ladies I have met are... well... not to be impolite, but they have all been rather dull. Not a one of them has ever refused a dance in favour of my friend." Her hand gripped his arm more tightly. "I understand your reasoning. There is no need to apologize."

"How did you know I was going to apologize?"

He shrugged. "You have a caring heart. I do not think you could knowingly harm another person."

"But I have!" she cried. "I was dreadful to Bea when I was at Heathcote."

"Knowingly dreadful?"

She nodded. "I felt it was not entirely right, and yet, I assisted Felicity in separating Bea from Mr. Everett Clayton."

"Why?"

"What do you mean?"

"Why did you persist in behaving as you were despite your misgivings?"

"Well, because Felicity assured me that I was being foolish to worry about such things, of course. She said it was how things were done, and that everyone understood that. That is exactly what she told me. That, and that she loved Mr. Everett Clayton most dearly – which she did not."

"You trusted your sister to guide you. There is nothing wrong in that."

Grace shook her head. "I will not allow it to be so. I should have listened to my heart and not my sister. I see that so clearly now."

"Seeing what has been is always easier than seeing what is."

Beside him, she sighed and very naturally, as if walking arm in arm with her closest friend, she squeezed his arm tight, which had the lovely effect of bringing a great deal more of her person in contact with him.

"You are very wise," she said.

Walter chuckled. "On occasion, but only on occasion. I reserve the right to be foolish and nonsensical when needed." The comment had the desired effect of eliciting a lovely laugh from her.

"When is it necessary to be nonsensical?" Grace asked between giggles.

"I really do not know, but I am certain there must be times when foolishness is preferable to being prudent." He leaned closer to her. "I will let you know when I discover such a time."

Again, the comment had the desired effect of causing her to continue to giggle.

"Shall we sit on this bench for a few minutes before we return and I must leave?"

They had come to the part of the garden where the path either circled back around toward the house or continued up a small set of stone steps and out into a portion of the garden that had been left quite rustic and natural. Here at the foot of those steps was a stone bench, tucked neatly off the path between two hedges and overshadowed by a tree, which when it bore leaves was a welcome respite from the sun. The bench itself was made of two stacks of stone, comprising the legs, and a large slab, spanning the distance between them. The slab, or seat, was well-worn from the many people who had sat upon it over the years.

"Do you know," Walter continued as Grace took a seat on the bench, "that this was my favourite place when I was just a lad and came to visit my grandparents."

"Was it really?" Grace smiled and ran a hand over the bit of slab next to her where he was about to sit. "It is a lovely bench, and the aspect from here is delightful." She leaned toward him when he finally took a seat. "I am particularly fond of arched garden gates, and you can see the gate between the hedges quite perfectly from here. I imagine that the gate is even more delightful when all the flowers are in bloom."

"It is," Walter agreed. "And when the tree behind us is laden with leaves, there is something very cozy feeling about this place, almost as if one could hide here, which I must say, I have."

"You have hidden here?"

Walter nodded. "When I was just a boy of about six, I used to curl into a ball under this very bench when playing hide-and-go-seek. Every time." He gave her a sheepish grin. "I would not advise using the same hiding place over and over if one has been found in it. It is the surest way to lose a game."

She giggled. He did so love hearing her do so. It was enough to make any of the uneasiness he felt at admitting such foolishness fade away.

"As I said, I am not always wise."

"No one is when he is six," she assured him. "Do you still hide here? Not under the bench. You would surely not fit there now, but by sitting here?"

He nodded. "I do not know if I would say I hide here now, but it is one of my favourite spots in all of the garden."

She turned toward him, angling her body so that she was not just turning her head. In doing so, her knee rested against the side of his leg. The action did not seem to bother her in the least. She seemed exceptionally comfortable with him. He, on the other hand, found it to be unexpectedly distracting in a very pleasant sort of fashion. So distracting in fact, that he shifted his leg away from her so that he might keep his mind where it should be.

"Why do you not live here? Erondale is your house, is it not?"

"It is," he replied as he shifted to look more fully at her but taking care to keep from touching her. "I am only one person. What do I need with so large a house?"

"But you could sit here every day if you lived here."

"True, but I can command a higher rent for Erondale than I can for my townhouse, and currently, I would rather have more money and live in my townhouse where I am steps from all that there is to do in Bath. I fear I would find spending my evenings at Erondale to be dreadfully boring with only myself to keep me company."

She looked toward the house. "It would be a difficult thing to choose between the beauty here and the excitement of town," she agreed. "What will you do when you marry?" She was looking at him again and her cheeks bore a rosy hue while she attempted to looked serene, though she was doing a very poor job of it.

"I will likely rent out my townhouse and take up residence here. That is, of course, unless my wife wishes to live in town. However, after there are children, this garden would be just the thing for them." He tipped his head and studied her face for a moment. "What would you do? If you were the owner of Erondale and a townhouse in Bath?"

"I would have to know what the townhouse looks like to make an accurate decision, but if it is as nice or nicer than the one which Father has rented, I would be tempted to stay in town for a time — although I do love Erondale and this garden, and the shops are not too far a drive away."

"But it all hinges on the townhouse?" He was quite certain she would like his home in town. He had not taken some small place that suited his needs as an unmarried gentleman. He had taken a townhouse that was both in a desirable location and had rooms enough for a family, for he knew that one day he would be renting it out and so, he had invested accordingly.

She nodded.

"Well, then," he said as he rose and held out his hand to assist her in rising, "you shall have to visit me in town at some point."

Her eyes grew wide as she stood before him. Close enough that if he put his arm out — just so. He could wrap it around her back and pull her to him – like that.

"In case," he said, looking down into her eyes and seeing once again that delectable look of longing, "in case, somewhere along the way during this courtship, we decide we suit."

Her tongue flicked out, moistening her lips, while she nodded mutely. It was nearly an invitation he could not resist. Nearly.

"Forgive me," he whispered as he released her from his embrace. "I have taken liberties where I should not have."

Her disappointment was written clearly on her face. "Please, I..." She shrugged as if she was not certain what she wanted to say. "You may kiss me," she offered quietly. Her chest was lifting and lowering with deliberate breaths just as his was.

"Not yet," he said above the hammering of his heart in his ears. When had holding a lady ever caused his heart to thud so loudly? When had he ever desired a kiss so much as he did at this moment?

"When?" she whispered.

He lifted her hand to his lips and kissed it. "Perhaps, one day," he said as he tucked the hand he had kissed into the crook of his arm. "Perhaps, one day."

Chapter 9

A full day and several hours later, the lingering effects of an almost first kiss had not worn off. Such an intimate moment was a heady thing, and Grace could not put the memory of such wonderfulness by without giving it the full amount of respect it was due. This, of course, required a wistful sigh upon each remembrance. Since Mr. Blakesley had departed Erondale yesterday, it had honestly been a struggle of nearly herculean proportions for Grace to think of much else besides how it had felt to be held by him. Oh, it had been most delightful! How did one feel such perfectness in the arms of a gentleman and still entertain thoughts of others? Grace simply could not fathom how her sister could do so. Felicity really was beyond understanding.

"What is that sigh?" Victoria whispered. "I have

heard it several times both yesterday and today. Is all well?"

"Yes, all is perfect. Can you believe we are here? This room is so lovely, and I just know the music will be divine, do you not think so?" And Mr. Blakesley would join them – along with Mr. Norman, of course. But even if he was to be a full chair away from her, she would get to see him and speak with him. Turning from Victoria to survey the room once more and peek yet again at the doorway in hopes of seeing Mr. Blakesley arrive, she was surprised to find that very gentleman standing behind his friend near the empty seats beside her.

"You look lovely this evening," Mr. Norman said. "May I sit with you?" He looked past her to Graeme, who nodded.

"Good evening, Mr. Norman and Mr. Blakesley." Grace tried to keep her eyes mostly on Mr. Norman, but it was excessively difficult to ignore Mr. Blakesley. This scheme was going to be most trying for that very reason.

"Good evening, Miss Grace," Mr. Blakesley replied. "Mr. Norman insisted I join him in attending tonight's concert. I hope you do not mind the imposition?" Small crinkles formed near his eyes which were filled with amusement.

Grace had never thought that lines around one's eyes could be so lovely as they were when he smiled at her. "I do not mind in the least. It is a grand thing to have a large group of friends to keep one company. Would you not agree, Mr. Norman?"

"Yes, yes. Quite so." He leaned forward. "And how are you this evening, Mrs. Shelton?"

"I am well, thank you. As is Mrs. Clayton."

"That is good news."

Mr. Norman's smile was relaxed and easy. He truly did care about the wellbeing of others. Grace looked around the room as he continued to speak to Mr. and Mrs. Shelton about their day and the weather and a few other things. Surely, in this vast array of people, there must be one lady who would like to marry a handsome and kind physician.

"Grace!"

Her eyes closed as the wonderfulness of the evening was sucked from her with that one word.

"Mama, look. It is Grace."

"Indeed, it is, and Beatrice and Mr. Clayton," Mrs. Love replied. "And several others I have yet to meet," she added with a quick glance at Mr. Norman and a raised eyebrow for Grace.

"I am well," Grace replied, causing her mother to look somewhat chagrinned.

"I am delighted to hear that. I was just about to inquire after your health and that of dear Bea." With a few *pardon me*'s, Mrs. Love and Felicity, followed by Mr. Love and Mr. Ramsey, squeezed past those already seated in the row in front of Grace so that they could sit just in front of Mr. and Mrs. Shelton and Mr. and Mrs. Clayton.

Having gained her seat, Mrs. Love turned to Bea. "How are you, my dear? I have been concerned about you. There is so much commotion in Bath and all that."

"I am no worse than normal," Bea answered. "Tonight will wear on me, but tomorrow is to be devoted to quiet pursuits."

Grace was not certain if what Bea said was true. It had seemed to her that Bea was finding it impossible to make it through a single day without retiring for a rest. She had never done so at Heathcote last year.

"As long as the times of reprieve outweigh the

times of exertion, no ill will befall her," Mr. Clayton said.

Could any gentleman look more pleased with his wife than Mr. Clayton did right now? It was enough to elicit one more small sigh from Grace, which in turn earned Grace a furrowed, worried brow look from Victoria.

"He is just so good to her," Grace whispered.

Victoria smiled and patted Grace's hand in way of agreement.

"It is a relief to hear it, is it not, Mr. Love?" Grace's mother said.

"A great relief," Mr. Love said with a wink for Bea. "Now, if my wife is done, perhaps we can have some introductions."

And so, the Sheltons, as well as Mr. Norman and Mr. Blakesley were introduced by Graeme to the Loves and Mr. Ramsey. And, in turn, Mr. Ramsey was introduced by Mr. Love to the Claytons and Mr. Norman and Mr. Blakesley, since he was already known by the Sheltons.

"A man of medicine?" Mrs. Love asked as if she had never heard of such a thing about Mr. Norman before. "That is a handy friend to have." She smiled at Bea.

"Oh, he is more than handy," Mr. Blakesley said. "He is one of the most loyal friends a fellow could find. He has done me more than one good turn for very little in return."

"And he is very well-liked," Grace added. "I am certain you did not make it into the room without being stopped by several people eager to wish you a good evening." She looked expectantly at Mr. Norman whose brow furrowed for a moment.

"We spoke to four individuals and their parties before we had even reached the door to this room," Mr. Blakesley said, much to Grace's relief. Thankfully, it seemed one of her companions understood the need to praise Mr. Norman to her mother.

"I suppose I am so used to being stopped that I did not even consider it as something about which to keep account," Mr. Norman added. "It is a hazard of my profession, I suppose."

"I shall have to disagree," Mr. Blakesley said. "Norman here would have just as many well-wishers no matter his profession. He is just the sort of fellow who makes friends with ease."

"He does seem so," Grace agreed.

"The same could be said about Blakesley," Roger

inserted. "Therefore, it makes sense that you should be such good friends."

"And how do you know Mr. Shelton?" Grace's father asked of Mr. Blakesley.

"We attended school together," Graeme answered. "The three of us."

No more was able to be said as the concert was set to begin. At least, no words were able to be spoken. However, Mrs. Love could not refrain from sending a speaking glance Grace's direction several times during the performance. Therefore, when the music had stopped and the crowds began to mill about and make their way out of the room, albeit slowly, Grace was not surprised at all to find her mother at her elbow.

"Does Mr. Blakesley have an estate?" she whispered.

"Yes, it is the one Mr. Clayton and Mr. Shelton have leased."

"And is it large?"

Grace shook her head. "Not overly so. It is quite perfectly proportioned. The gardens are well-designed, and the house does not want for care."

"He is handsome."

The hopeful note in her mother's tone caused

Grace's stomach to tumble. "But what of Mr. Ramsey?" she asked, putting her anxious thoughts into words.

"Oh, I am not inquiring for Felicity." Her mother looked at her expectantly. "An estate owner is a better choice than a physician," she added when Grace said nothing.

Grace had not held her tongue purposefully. Her mind was whirling, attempting to keep her scheme in her control rather than having it overtaken by any of her mother's matchmaking attempts. It would not matter if their mother had arranged things to Grace's advantage. Grace could see how Felicity even now, while standing with her hand on Mr. Ramsey's arm was assessing Mr. Blakesley, and Grace would not allow Mr. Blakesley to be snatched from her like Mr. Everett Clayton and Mr. Ramsey had been.

"He is not unattached," she whispered to her mother. Her heart thudded, heavy and fast within her chest. "There is a lady who has captured Mr. Blakesley's attention.

"I do not see anyone on his arm," her mother countered.

"That is because she is not here. She is not even in Bath."

"She is not?" There was a great deal of interest mixed with surprise in the question. "If she is not here, then, where is she?"

Grace's brow furrowed. Where was this imaginary lady from? "Um, I think..." A smile curled her lips as the perfect reply became obvious. Surely, any gentleman who had nearly kissed a lady must have had his attention captured by that lady. "I think she is from Kent."

"Near us?" her mother asked, casting a furtive look in Mr. Blakesley's direction.

"I could not say." Because the lady was very, very near their estate in Kent. In fact, she was a resident at that estate. However, her mother could not know that.

"What is her name?"

Grace shook her head. "I am sure I could not tell you. I have only heard bits and pieces, and I did not think it polite to ask."

Her mother looked disappointed. "I suppose that is true, unfortunately." She sighed. "Do you know if he is betrothed?"

"I do not believe he is." *Oh! That was the wrong*

thing to say, Grace scolded herself as her mother's face brightened.

"If he is not betrothed, then there could be no harm in a wee mite of flirting."

"Mama, I am not Felicity."

Her mother gasped and looked affronted.

"I will not attempt to steal a gentleman from another," Grace clarified.

"I was not saying you should, of course. I was just thinking that if you were to flirt with him a trifle, we might find out how attached he is to this young woman."

"That sounds a great deal like attempting to steal him from another," Grace answered. "I will not do it."

"Oh, very well. I suppose you are correct. But an estate owner is so much better than a physician."

"Mr. Norman is a very kind man, Mama."

Mrs. Love sighed. "But kindness does not put food on the table."

"It is far more likely that kindness will before unkindness does."

"Oh, Grace," her mother chided. "You know what I mean. I cannot say your father will approve of such a match."

"Please, Mother, could we speak of something else?" Anything else. There were two older ladies who were watching them closely. With any luck, they would both be hard of hearing and would not have heard a word of her discussion with her mother.

"Mr. Blakesley," her mother said as she pulled Grace forward. "Grace was telling me that you have a young lady waiting for you in Kent, and since we are from Kent, I do hope that you will call on us when you are there."

Grace's eyes grew wide. Her mother was not supposed to mention this imaginary lady to Mr. Blakesley!

"You are from Kent?" he replied with all the calm of a gentleman surveying a billiard table. There was a calculating look to his expression and small quizzical lift to his left eyebrow when he glanced at Grace.

"Yes, has Grace not told you?"

"I am afraid we have not had a great deal of time to discuss such things."

Grace pressed her lips together to keep from smiling. That was a bald-faced lie, and though she did not normally approve of such things, presently, she found it very well done.

"Well, then," her mother said with a coy smile of her own, "I would not be opposed to a call so that we can learn more about one another. It would be a great boon to have another person from Kent to count as a friend."

"I am not from Kent, nor will I ever be," Mr. Blakesley interrupted.

"Yes, yes, but your young lady. I would be delighted to know about her and her family."

Mr. Blakesley opened his mouth to protest further but Mrs. Love, rather pointedly, paid him no mind and continued on.

"Of course, if you do not wish to call on me to discuss such things, I am certain Grace would be able to do an admirable job of acquainting you with our family. You could accompany your friend, Mr. Norman, when he calls on Grace." Her lashes fluttered twice.

Embarrassment washed over Grace. "Mama," she whispered. Could her mother be any less circumspect about her motives?

Mr. Blakesley's lips tipped up ever so slightly. "I suppose that will be entirely up to Mr. Norman, madame. However, I dare say even his kind nature will not allow me to interfere with his purpose regarding your daughter." He looked at Grace. "I know I would not let anyone, whether gentleman or lady, divide me from such a lovely prize if I were Mr. Norman." His gaze held hers for the briefest of moments, but long enough to inform her that he was not speaking in hypothetical terms. "And speaking of that good friend, I am going to have to snatch him away from Mr. Shelton, since we travelled together, for I have an early day tomorrow and would like to find my pillow quite soon. Good night, ladies. It has been a pleasure." He bowed first over Mrs. Love's hand and then, Grace's, giving her fingers the tiniest of squeezes as he did.

"He is a lovely young man," Mrs. Love said longingly as she watched him leave.

And for once, Grace had to admit that her mother was perfectly correct.

Chapter 10

"Mr. Blakesley, what a delightful surprise to see you here."

Walter, who had risen quickly and found himself a seat other than beside Grace when it was noted that Mrs. Love had arrived, bowed and extended his welcome.

"Is Mr. Norman with you?" Mrs. Love glanced around the room.

"He was, but then he was called away," Grace answered.

"Yes, there was a patient in need of an urgent consultation," Walter added. "He has promised to return to collect me before night falls." Not that Walter cared one bit if he was forced to spend the night at his own estate. There were certain inducements which would make it quite pleasurable. Not only did he have friends and a well-stocked larder and wine cellar here at Erondale, there was also Grace.

Mrs. Love tsked. "Such a life. To be always at someone's beck and call." She gave her daughter a pointed look. Apparently, Grace had not exaggerated her mother's disdain for a physician as a possible husband for her daughter.

"I believe he enjoys it, Mama," Grace replied. "For he did not look put out in the least. I can imagine that being so very knowledgeable about all things pertaining to health and knowing that you might bring relief and help to another is quite fulfilling. Why if I were to be in possession of such knowledge, I am certain I would not mind one bit being asked to provide aide to another. As it is, you know how much I enjoy visiting those who are less fortunate."

"You do?" There was no little amount of shock in Mrs. Love's tone, which pricked Walter's curiosity.

He could see Grace being quite good at visiting those in need and lending her aide.

"I do." Grace smoothed her skirt. "I have just decided it."

Grace was also very good at vexing her mother.

Walter relaxed into his chair to watch the scene between mother and daughter unfold before him.

"You have?" Her mother still looked as if she were floundering in the sea without a hope of help.

"Yes. I find Mr. Norman to be very inspiring. If we were not in Bath, I would seek out the parson and discover if there is someone to whom I might be of service for an hour or two."

"You find Mr. Norman inspiring?"

"Very."

Walter bit back a grin at the look of utter delight Grace wore, which was in stark contrast to the ashen hue of her mother's face.

"But," Grace continued, "I suppose, I might find that I do not like being of service to the less fortunate as much as I imagine I might, and that would be dreadful in the extreme." Her brow furrowed. "I wonder if Mr. Norman would find me wanting if such were the case?"

"Yes, yes, I think he might," her mother hurried to assure her.

"Is Felicity not with you?"

Mrs. Love blinked at Grace's sudden shift of topics. "She was expecting a call from Mr. Ramsey."

"And you are letting her receive him without

yourself being present?" Graeme asked in astonishment.

Mrs. Love smiled slyly. "Her father is there, and I think Mr. Ramsey might wish to see Mr. Love rather than me."

Grace's face lit with excitement. "Do you really think he is going to offer for her?"

Something of great interest on the hem of Mrs. Love's glove captured her attention as she replied, "It is quite likely."

"And will she accept him?" From the wideness of Grace's eyes, Graeme's question surprised her as much as her mother.

"I do believe she will," Mrs. Love replied. "At least, we are hopeful."

"Will she marry in Bath? How quickly do you think it could be accomplished?" Grace asked eagerly.

Mrs. Love laughed. "I think we shall leave some of those details up to the happy couple to decide."

"But to be married in the Abbey would be something worthy of note to all Felicity's friends. Do you not think?" Grace bit her lip anxiously.

Walter had known Grace was eager to have her

sister settled, but he had not thought her quite so eager as she appeared at this moment.

"It would be noteworthy," her mother agreed. "But there is no rush."

Grace's shoulders slumped. "Can my season begin before she is Mrs. Ramsey? Or must I wait until after she marries."

"She will still need to be seen in company, and I do not see why she cannot enjoy a few more festivities as Miss Love before she becomes Mrs. anyone."

Grace sighed and slumped down in her seat. "I should like to have a season before I marry," she said softly.

"Ah, but if you marry Mr. Norman," Mr. Blakesley said, "you will have the delights of Bath at your door. Your life can be a continual season. That would be a definite advantage to having a husband who lives in Bath."

Mrs. Love looked at him in horror, and he thought for a moment that Grace was going to giggle. However, she refrained. Roger did not. He chuckled while his wife discreetly captured his hand and, most likely, gave it a squeeze to remind the fellow that he was not to find the conversation so entertaining.

"I suppose it is." Grace sighed loudly. "Then, Felicity may marry whenever she wishes."

"A wedding in the Abbey would be noteworthy," her mother said, this time with a great deal more conviction than she had the first time.

"A double ceremony would be even more noteworthy," Roger said as he shot a quick glance in Walter's direction.

It was a thought worthy of consideration. He tilted his head and studied Grace. Grace Blakesley? It had a pleasing ring to it. However, the double ceremony would never happen. Grace deserved her own day, far removed from her sister. She had lived in that shadow long enough.

"No, no," Mrs. Love said, "one wedding at a time will be trying enough. And I am certain Grace is not yet ready to marry."

"I might be," Grace said.

"It is not a thing to be rushed into," Mrs. Clayton said softly.

"Oh, goodness, no!" Grace agreed.

"However, if one meets the right gentleman and falls in love with him and he with her, then is it rushing?" Walter asked, keeping his eyes on Mrs.

Clayton and not allowing them to roam to Grace as they wished to do.

"I would say no," Graeme answered.

"I would agree," Roger said.

"What of the ladies? What do you think on this matter?" Walter asked.

"This imaginary couple is truly in love?" Mrs. Shelton asked.

Walter nodded. "They would give all they had to see the other happy."

"Then, no, if they are certain they are in love and do not just fancy themselves so, I would say it is not rushing."

"I think I would agree if that is the case," Mrs. Clayton said.

Walter turned to Mrs. Love.

"I do not think I wish to answer that," she said, lifting her chin. "I shall leave it up to Mr. Love to decide if it is rushing."

Walter had to admit that hers was the perfect answer, for if she had said she did not think it was rushing, it would have given her daughter, whom she feared thought herself enamoured with the unacceptable Mr. Norman, freedom to run pell-mell into marriage with the fellow. However, by deferring to her husband, who was not present, she allowed room for the delay of an untenable marriage and avoided any present argument with her daughter.

"He would give all he had to see her happy?" Grace asked when Walter turned to her for her answer.

Walter nodded. "And she would do the same for him."

"Even if it led to misery?"

"Or death," Walter added.

"Oh, my."

He had never seen Grace look so very serious.

"Is that how you feel about your husbands?" Her eyes shifted to Mrs. Shelton and Mrs. Clayton, who both nodded. "And you about your wives?" she asked Graeme and Roger, who also nodded. Her brow furrowed, and she turned to her mother. "And that is how you feel about Father?"

Mrs. Love glanced around the room, her cheeks growing the faintest bit rosy. "Well, that is rather dramatic, and I am not one to be dramatic."

Walter doubted that. He had seen her daughters, and both appeared to him to be perfectly capable of dramatics.

"However," she continued, "I suppose that is how I feel about your father."

"The question remains, Miss Grace," Walter pressed. Her answer was the most important one in the room. "If those were the conditions, do you think it would be rushing to marry in haste?"

She sat quietly for a moment before her lips curled upward. "I suppose that would depend on what the gentleman who loved me thought, for if I am willing to live in misery on his behalf, then if waiting to marry, which might prove miserable, is what would make him happy, I would have no option but to defer to his desire. If I did otherwise, would that not prove I did not love him as deeply as I should?"

That was not an answer he had expected her to give. "I had not thought of it so," he admitted.

"But does this gentleman know that making you wait would make you miserable?" Roger asked. "Would that not then call his own devotion to you into question?"

A pained expression created a great furrow between Grace's eyes. "Then, how is one ever to know if one is in love enough to marry?"

"That is an excellent question," Roger replied,

turning to Walter. "Do you have an explanation? You always had some reply when we pondered such impossible things in school."

Walter shook his head. "I am afraid my answer will not be satisfying, for I think that love is not something which can be dissected into bits and pieces to be analyzed for proof of existence. Not that it cannot be examined and found to exist."

"I am terribly confused," Grace said.

Walter smiled at her. "I think that one just simply knows, and that, for each person, the item of proof differs despite some similarities in all cases."

"You are very wise," Mrs. Love inserted.

"Thank you," Walter answered, though his eyes did not leave her daughter.

"And have you found that measure of proof with your lady?" Mrs. Love prodded.

Had he? Was it not too soon to have discovered such a thing? He had not known Grace for more than a handful of days, though he had known *of* her for a few days before that. He shrugged. "I am not entirely certain."

"You are not?" Mrs. Love sounded eager as if she was hoping he would give up this lady whom she did not know was her daughter.

"No, I am not. Though," his heart beat a bit faster as he considered giving Grace up to another gentleman, "I dare say I could not be persuaded away from choosing her." And within the walls of that thought lay the truth. His heart belonged to his mysterious angel – even if it did feel a bit as if he was rushing into something – something which, he suspected, would be quite wonderful.

Chapter 11

"We could sit under this tree." Grace suggested when she, Bea and Victoria were taking a stroll through Sydney Gardens two days later.

Bea was looking rather tired, causing Grace to worry about her. She would hate for her cousin to become ill, and not just because it would mean they would have to forego their plans for the evening. She was finding it quite delightful to have friends such as Bea and Victoria, and she desired to demonstrate her care for them as much as they seemed willing to do for her.

Graeme and Roger had left the three of them to take a walk while they went to see a tailor about a... Grace's face scrunched. They had gone to see the tailor about something, but for the life of her, she could not recall what it was. That was likely because she had been too occupied with looking at

Mr. Blakesley...Walter... She sighed as she thought his name. She still had not decided what she would call him in private, but she did enjoy using his Christian name when thinking about him.

"If we sit there, we could indulge in our buns," Victoria agreed. "I find I am once again hungry and being hungry does not bode well for my ability to keep my stomach right side up."

"Are you also unwell?" Grace turned her attention from her cousin, who was beginning to look pale, to her friend who did not look at all unwell. However, both her friend and her cousin had been ill several times over the past few days. It was odd really. No one else had become ill, and the illness had not settled in, forcing either lady to take to her bed for an extended period of time.

"No, not at present," Victoria said to Grace before turning to smile at Bea. "We should sit. It would most certainly not be the thing for you to cast up our accounts or swoon in the garden."

"Oh, not at all!" Grace cried.

"Graeme would never allow me out of the house or his sight again if he were to learn of it," Bea said.

Victoria laughed. "I was more concerned with being a spectacle, but I think my husband would be the same." She took a seat on the ground and smoothed her skirts. "And being confined to the house would be no way to experience Bath."

"Is the ground dry?" Grace asked. She did not wish to ruin the skirt of her dress as she had only just received this one from Felicity who had been seen enough times wearing it on walks.

"Yes, and it is not too very cold either since it has had the sun to warm it this morning," Victoria assured her.

There was still a bit of sun shining on the ground, though the sun was beginning to find its way to the other side of the tree under which they sat.

"This must be a lovely place for a picnic when the leaves are all out," Grace commented as she took a seat.

"Perhaps one day you will be so fortunate as to have a picnic here," Bea said with a smile. "Mr. Blakesley is a wonderful match, and I do believe he is intent on convincing you of that very thing."

"I do hope so," the words popped out of Grace's mouth before she had a moment to think about them. "Or, at least, I think I do," she corrected.

"You do not need to pretend with us," Victoria assured her.

"I am not pretending," Grace replied. "I am not certain if I should hope for such an eventuality or not." She shook her head. "No, that is not it. I am quite certain I could like Mr. Blakesley very well for the rest of my life. However, I am not certain if I should know if I could or not just yet." She looked at the confused faces of her companions and added, "I do not know if I would give up everything for him. I have been considering it since his call two days ago, and I think that I would. However, how can I know for sure unless I have been faced with the possibility?"

Victoria laughed. "I think the fact that you are thinking about it so carefully likely proves that it is not too soon to hope to be Mrs. Blakesley at some point."

"He is as upstanding as he appears," Bea added. "Graeme has been doing some investigating," she whispered.

"He has?" That was surprising.

"He would not want you to be taken in by a scoundrel," Bea answered. "He is taking his role of guardian to you while in our company quite seriously." She rested a hand on her stomach. "He will be a good father to our children – which, of course, I knew, but of which I am happy to be reminded."

Grace's brow furrowed. Was Bea hinting at what she thought Bea was hinting? She glanced at the hand on Bea's stomach.

"Yes," Bea whispered, her cheeks growing a tad rosy.

"You are going to have a baby?"

"You cannot tell anyone," Bea cautioned. "Not yet. Not until things are more firmly undeniable. I have yet to feel any movement, and I will feel much better sharing the news with one and all once that has occurred."

"I think with how ill you and I have been, there is little doubt that we are pregnant."

"You, too!" Grace cried, turning toward Victoria, who nodded. "This is why you have been tired and unwell?"

Again, Victoria nodded.

"And why you have seen Mr. Norman so often?"

"Yes," Bea said. "Graeme is far more concerned about my health than is necessary, but it is sweet."

"He is so solicitous." Grace clapped her hands together once but then, put them in her lap rather than clapping more as she wished to do. She had just been trusted with a great secret. Therefore, she was not about to draw attention to them by being overly exuberant. "This is such good news! When is the happy event to take place?" She tried to keep her tone interested but not excited.

"The end of summer," Victoria said. "For both of us, according to Mr. Norman's calculations."

"How exciting! You will have children who will be the same age. They will be such good friends, just as Mr. Shelton and Mr. Clayton are and how the two of you are as well." They would no doubt spend a great deal of time visiting one another for Grace could not imagine Graeme and Roger being separated for too overly long a period of time.

"It is a lovely thought," Bea said. "And one which I hold close."

"It is wonderful, simply wonderful," Grace said as she broke off a piece of her bun. "These are enormous," she muttered.

"And delicious," Victoria added.

Victoria was not wrong. Having tasted her first bite of a Sally Lunn, it was obvious to Grace why Walter liked them so well. In fact, it was he who had brought the delectable treats to them today.

If she were to marry him, these delectable treats could be a frequent visitor to her table. She closed her eyes and savoured the taste of her bun and the thought of being Mrs. Blakesley.

"This is quite the lovely sight."

Grace opened her eyes to see Mr. Blakesley standing before her.

"Indeed, it is," Roger agreed.

Grace pulled her eyes away from Walter long enough to see that both Roger and Graeme had returned.

"You may join us," Grace offered. "There is plenty of this bun for sharing. I am certain I should not eat the full thing."

"And why should you not?" Walter did not wait to be convinced to take a seat next to her. He rather swiftly claimed the bit of ground to her right and accepted the portion of bun she gave him. "They are delicious."

"Oh, indeed, they are," Grace assured him. "However, if I were to eat an entire bun every day – as I quite wish to do – I would have to be rolled through the garden since I would likely grow very round."

The responding laughter from Walter was delightfully pleasing.

"You are sounding a bit like Mr. Norman," he cautioned.

"How so?" Grace asked.

"He is forever telling me that I should not indulge in these as often as I do." He popped a second morsel of the sweet roll into his mouth.

Warmth spread across Grace's cheeks as she envied the fingers from which he kissed away every trace of bun. That was most improper. She focused her eyes on the bun she held. "Do you eat them very often then?"

"As often as I can, which is nearly every day."

"The whole thing? Every day?" How did he not grow fat? Her mother had always scolded that indulging in sweets of any sort rather than vegetables and meat only lead to being fat and gouty.

He nodded as his fortunate fingers once again were kissed free of any morsels of sweetness. "That is why I walk far more often than I ride, and why I have taken up pugilism. Exercise balances the indulgence – or so Mr. Norman assures me. Therefore, if you were to say, dance a set or two with me this evening, that should compensate for the extravagance of this treat."

"I cannot dance with you." As much as she would like to do just that.

"One dance would not cause any stir. Your mother knows we are acquainted. In fact, to not dance with you would seem suspiciously rude."

"He has a point," Roger inserted.

"But my sister –"

"Will never pose an issue," Walter said.

"You do not know that," Grace argued.

"I think I do." He held her gaze most intently.

Oh, she wanted to dance with him! She truly did. She also wanted to believe that Felicity would never come between them, but at present, she was not certain she could trust her sister at all. Why just think of how Felicity had treated her!

"Trust me," he whispered. "Please."

"One set?" How could she refuse him when he looked so desirous of her granting him his wish?

He nodded.

"Not the first. That one should really go to Mr. Norman if he is there."

"Does that mean I may have one of the other sets?" Pleasure danced in his eyes.

"Yes, but only one set and only as a friend of a friend."

"If that is how you wish it to be. I will remind you, however, that your sister will never sway me to pay her any particular attention."

"I cannot trust her," Grace said softly.

"You do not have to. You need only trust me."

"One set," she replied. "We would not wish for your lady in Kent to hear of more than that and become jealous."

He chuckled. "She has no need to fear being made jealous."

"Right, well," Graeme interrupted. "If we are to get to the Assembly Rooms at all today, we must finish our walk and make certain these ladies have had ample time to rest and recover before preparing for a ball."

"Which is no small feat," Roger agreed with a laugh.

"Are you ready to go on?" Grace whispered to Bea who was on her left.

"Has she been unwell?" Graeme asked.

"No, no," Grace rushed to assure him. "She was a bit tired and... hungry," she added after taking note of Bea's half-eaten bun.

"Are you certain?" Graeme asked.

Grace nodded vigorously as Bea assured her husband that she was well. There was no way Grace wanted to miss either that dance with Walter or the dinner party which had been cunningly arranged so that she could see his townhouse.

"There are rooms at my home just waiting to be filled," Walter said as he rose and extended his hand to Grace. "The maids will be perfectly put out if they went to the bother to prepare them, and then they are not used. And Norman will be joining us later if there is a need for any tonics or tinctures. Although," he continued as he helped Grace to her feet and slipped her hand into the crook of his arm, "I have some peppermint leaves from which we can make a tea – not too strong, mind you – and then when it is cooled, you can try it for any relief it might impart. Or I have some oil which you can use for a headache."

Roger chuckled. "You sound very little like a bachelor, and more like a mother hen."

"Ah, the dangers of having Mr. Norman for a friend, I am afraid," Walter answered with a laugh. "I have learned much from him – some of it willingly even." Again, he laughed. "In all seriousness, a gentleman could not find a better friend than Norman." He glanced down at Grace. "Unless, of course, he gets two sets while I only have one."

"I must make a show of being enamoured with him," Grace argued. That was the crux of the plan. She was to pretend to wish for Mr. Norman's attentions while in truth it was Mr. Blakesley who was her true beau.

"I do not believe you do."

Grace sighed. "But that is the plan."

"Plans can change," Walter retorted.

"I know they can," Grace agreed. And she knew that someday her plan would need to change, but today was not that day, no matter how much Mr. Blakesley argued it should be. While she might be able to trust him, Felicity, the reason for the plan in the first place, was another matter altogether.

Chapter 12

"This is it," Walter said as Graeme's carriage drew to a stop in front of a town house in the middle of a row of houses standing on the eastern side of a square. "It is not overly grand," he said as he stood on the walkway that crossed over to the door. "However, it is of ample size for a small family."

"It is lovely," Victoria said.

"Yes, very," Grace agreed.

Walter could tell by the way she scanned the front of the building, tipping her head to see up it as high as possible, while smiling broadly, that she was duly impressed.

"If you look below us, there is a small courtyard and some storage with an entrance to the servants' quarters, as well as the kitchen and such."

"How do they get down there to enter?" Grace asked.

"There is a true entry at the rear of the house. I suppose I should have more accurately stated that there is an exit from the servants' quarters for access to the courtyard and storage."

"Ah," she said with a nod of her head as she continued to look at the courtyard and then once again moved her gaze to the façade of the house. "It is not very old, is it?"

He shook his head. "No, it not much older than you."

"Indeed? Is it very modern within?"

"I shall let you determine that." He waved his hand toward the door which stood, waiting for them to enter. He smiled at her exclamation upon entering just ahead of him.

"I believe she likes it," Graeme muttered behind him.

"I would say you are correct." And Walter was as delighted by that fact as Grace was by the flooring and the second door that separated the foyer from the interior of the house. He had hoped she would like his house, for he was beginning to hope quite seriously that it would one day also be hers.

They passed through the second door and stood in front of the staircase with two doors to the right of them and a third past the staircase and down the hall. It was through this door that a footman was disappearing with the various articles of outerwear he had gathered from Walter's guest.

"Your maid will be given what she needs," he said softly to Grace who was watching the footman.

"Oh, I have no doubt of that."

The smile she turned on him caused him to forget for a moment what he had intended to show them next. Thankfully, his mind did not fail him for long – only long enough for Roger to cough.

It was all well and good for him to be laughing at Walter's expense. The man was married and utterly besotted with his wife. It was not as if Walter was acting the part of a smitten swain on his own. It was just that he did not have the assurance that the object of his affection would always be at his side as both Roger and Graeme did.

He raised an eyebrow and gave Roger a challenging look that was met with a smirk and a nod of acceptance. Both of the men with him knew how important this evening was to Walter. He had made certain they knew on their walk to the tailor.

"Through here," Walter opened the first door to

his right, "we have the dining room. You may peek in, but since we will be spending time there later, there really is no need to enter. We do not wish to be underfoot," he added.

Within, one maid was using a small brush to sweep the chairs while another was placing a cloth on a table that stood near the table and would receive many of the serving utensils.

"And this door," he had moved to the second door which was only separated from the first by the space of a wall, "leads to my study." He stepped inside and the others followed.

"It is as organized as I would have expected," Roger said. "Blakesley was not the sort to ever have anything out of place in his lodgings," he explained. "You could ask him for anything and within a few moments, he would have it for you for he knew just where it should be."

"That seems like an excellent way to be," Bea said.

"Clayton and Shelton were also fairly well organized. Clayton more so than Shelton."

"I could see that," Grace said.

"You could?" Roger said.

Grace nodded. "You are a trifle more carefree

than Mr. Clayton. He is not stodgy, mind you, but he does have a more fatherly air about him." She shrugged. "Or so it seemed to me when I was at Heathcote, but then, I might just be thinking so from the way he was always scolding his brother and asking after Bea's wellbeing."

"My brother is an idiot," Graeme retorted. "If he were not, there would be no need to scold."

"I do not find him to be an idiot," Grace retorted and then shrugged. "If I did, I would also have to call myself one since I was just as duped as he was by my sister, and frankly, I do not wish to even think that word about myself. I will allow that we were both foolish."

"I did not mean to imply that you were an idiot," Graeme apologized. "But trust me, there have been many things over the years which Everett has done to earn the moniker."

"That is because he is your brother," Bea inserted. "To the rest of us, he is not so bad as he is to you."

"He treated you very ill," Graeme retorted.

"And look where that has led," Roger said.

And that one statement was all that was needed to silence Graeme about the idiocy of his brother.

In fact, much to Walter's amusement, before they had left the study, Graeme had begun to think that perhaps his brother's lack of sense was one of his best qualities.

"Has anyone asked you about the picture on our desk yet?" Grace asked as they climbed the stairs to the first floor.

She had stood behind his desk, picked up the framed silhouette he had drawn, smiled her secret smile at it and then him, and then returned it to its place.

"Not yet," he replied. "I only just got it back with the frame yesterday. I have not yet had time to have anyone ask."

"Are we not stopping on this floor?" she asked when he turned toward the second flight of stairs.

"We will return to it."

She stood at the bottom of the stairs and looked at him as if that was the most foolish thing she had ever heard.

"The drawing room and billiards room is on this floor. We will return to it after I have seen you settled in your accommodations."

Her brow furrowed and her lips puckered with displeasure.

"I promise."

"Very well," she said with a small huff. "But I am a curious creature."

"As am I," he assured her when she had reached the step on which he stood. "This next floor is mine. There is my bedchamber, a sitting room, and a dressing room. Do you wish to see it?"

"I think we can do without," Graeme said.

Walter chuckled. Grace was correct about Graeme having a fatherly air about him. "I assure you I have no intention of doing more than show-ing the rooms to Miss Grace." That lady gasped, while Roger chuckled, and Graeme cleared his throat and glared at Walter.

"Our rooms?" Graeme said.

"Are on the next floor. There are two rooms of substantial size and two smaller rooms. I have instructed that the larger rooms be readied for you and Shelton, while one of the smaller rooms has been made ready for Miss Grace." He opened doors and assigned people to each room. Then, he made to leave them. "I will be in the drawing room or my study if you should need me."

Grace turned to enter her room, but not before sharing one more of her secret smiles with him. If he had deduced things correctly, Grace would not be long in finding her way to the drawing room which she had not been allowed to see.

And he was not wrong. No more than twenty minutes later, Grace stepped quietly into the drawing room. Alone.

He discarded the book he had been reading. "We have no chaperone," he cautioned.

"Am I not to trust you?" Her eyes danced with impertinence.

"I had hoped you would, but you seem hesitant to do so."

Her mouth popped open and then closed as her brow furrowed. "Do you mean about our scheme and not just now?"

"I do." He rose and motioned toward the windows. "The view of the park is excellent from here."

The comment drew her across the room to him.

"Oh, it is!"

"Those trees will one day be much larger, but there are several different specimens which add to the beauty of the autumn when the leaves show all their glory." He stood directly behind her. Almost of their own accord, his arms wrapped around her.

It was almost of their own accord because he had paused for a fraction of a moment to consider the action before undertaking it. True, it had not been long enough of a pause to consider much more than how wonderful it would be to hold her. To his delight, she did not jump or squeal, but instead, sighed and leaned back against him.

"This is not proper," she said.

"Indeed, it is not, and I am risking the ire of Clayton."

She nodded.

"He might even force me to offer for you if we are found thusly." He was not sure if his caution was for her or his own mind, which had begun to wonder how her neck might taste.

"What would you do if he did?" The question was barely more than a whisper.

"I would offer for you now, rather than later." He felt her sharp intake of breath. "I have come to the conclusion that I should very much like to offer for you at some point if you will allow it." His heart hammered against his ribs as if it was asking to be freed from the confines of his body. This was not part of how he had planned this evening to go. He was rushing forward when he should be holding back and giving her time to come to trust him enough to be seen with him in public without the ruse of being merely a friend before making any sort of offer. He swallowed and, despite his trepidation, pressed on. "Do I have a hope of ever being allowed?"

Her hands covered his where they were clasped against her stomach. She rubbed them gently as the silence following his question grew longer. Finally, she spoke.

"I want to say yes."

His heart sank. She was rejecting him.

"However, I am not certain." She turned in his arms to look at him. "I have only just learned what love is. I had not thought it so all-consuming as it appears to be." She tilted her head. "Could I give up my happiness for yours?" She shrugged. "I should like to think so, but..." She shook her head.

"You are uncertain?"

She nodded. "And I would hate myself forever if I were to promise you my heart only to discover later that I was mistaken." Her eyes glistened. "I have seen the harm such a thing can do, and I could never harm you in such a fashion."

His heart thrilled at her admission. She was not

rejecting him out of hand. In fact, her words proved that, unbeknownst to her, she was well on her way to being in love with him. He ran the back of his right hand along her jaw, and then passed a finger over her tempting lips. How he long to kiss them! However, they were not his to claim just yet.

"Then, I suppose we should not be caught standing as we are, for I would not wish to be the cause of your unhappiness." He passed his finger over her lips once more before pressing a kiss to her forehead and then releasing her before he allowed himself to do more.

"Do you like to read?" He turned from her, smiling at her disappointed sigh. "Or, I could teach you to play billiards."

"Could you really?" she asked eagerly.

He crossed to the door which joined the drawing room to the billiards room and opened it. Billiards would be far better than reading. He had told Grace that he was not the sort of gentleman to seduce a lady, and until this moment, he had not been. However, as her face lit with delight, he had to admit to himself that he most certainly planned to seduce Grace. Not so he could have the momentary pleasure of having her in his bed just once, but so he could win her heart and, in so doing, have her always in his bed, in his drawing room, at his table, as his dance partner for as many sets as he wished, in his arms as they stood looking over the park or admiring his garden at Erondale, and forever as his wife.

Chapter 13

"You make a charming couple," Mrs. Love whispered.

Grace sighed. There were many interesting places where her mother could see and be seen and hear any number of tantalizing tales, but instead of choosing one of those places to be, her mother had decided that the empty seat beside Grace was the perfect place to sit while Felicity danced.

"Have we any happy news?" Grace completely ignored her mother's comment about Mr. Blakesley, who had just danced the first set with Grace, and attempted to steer the conversation in a better direction.

Mrs. Love clucked her tongue. "Not yet, and I cannot imagine what is keeping him from coming to the point."

"He knows about Mr. Everett Clayton, you

know," Grace ducked her head close to her mother's ear. "Perhaps he is just being cautious?"

"How can he doubt her regard? Look at her." Mrs. Love motioned toward the floor with her fan. "She is smitten, simply smitten. Can you not see it in how she looks at him?"

Grace squinted her eyes and studied, really studied, her older sister but to no avail. She had seen Felicity look at Mr. Everett Clayton in that same way.

"One does not look so at a suitor unless one is hoping for an offer," Mrs. Love added.

One did if one was Felicity. No, that was not entirely true, Grace corrected. Her sister had wished for an offer from Mr. Everett Clayton until she had found something more to her liking.

"How do you know it is not just an act?"

"An act?" her mother repeated in surprise.

"Need I remind you that Felicity was smitten at Heathcote and remained so until the second day of the Abernathy's house party when Mr. Ramsey spoke to her."

The statement was met with a great exhalation of breath from Mrs. Love. "A mother knows," she answered.

Grace schooled her eyebrows to remain immobile rather than arching skeptically as they wished to do. "How precisely does a mother know?"

"I am certain I cannot distill it, but there is feeling." She laid her hand on her heart. "Your sister is more attached this time. I just know she is. There was a hesitance about Mr. Everett Clayton. I never once saw her smile wistfully while stitching as if she was thinking of Mr. Everett Clayton, but she does now. And when I asked her about it just yesterday, she sighed and said, 'Is he not the most perfect gentleman?'"

Grace was not completely convinced, but she was willing, upon hearing such a story, to allow that it might be possible for her sister to be, at long last, irrevocably attached to a gentleman. However, for herself, she would only be satisfied when she saw Felicity standing at the altar repeating her vows.

"I dare say you would not say Mr. Ramsey is the perfect gentleman."

Grace looked at her mother in feigned astonishment. "How do you mean?"

"Oh, come now, Grace. I would venture that Mr. Blakesley is a trifle more perfect in your estimation.

You were looking very content to be dancing with him."

"He is a friend. How could one not feel content while dancing with a friend?"

Her mother tipped her head and pursed her lips. It was a sure sign that she did not believe a word Grace was saying. And that was not good for Grace's scheme. Therefore, without much thought beyond needing to keep her ruse going and Mr. Blakesley safe from Felicity, she continued, "However, I do see your meaning now, and I would have to agree."

Her mother smiled smugly.

"Mr. Norman is far superior to Mr. Ramsey." She sighed for effect. "It really is too bad he was not here to dance the first set as he had promised. But one cannot predict, with any great deal of accuracy, when someone is going to fall ill."

"Mr. –" Her mother huffed as if she could not even bear to speak Mr. Norman's name. "Really, Grace. You cannot be serious. I do not know why you insist upon pursuing such a fellow. He seems an honorable sort of gentleman, I will give you that. But, Grace, your father and I did not send you to school to become a physician's wife! You will cease this foolishness."

"It is not foolishness," Grace insisted but her mother would not hear any explanation.

Instead, she rose. "I will find your father. See that your sister does not come to ruin in my absence."

Grace grabbed her mother's hand before she could leave. "You do not need to get Father. I admire Mr. Norman greatly, but I am not yet set on him."

Her mother looked down at Grace. "You are not?"

Grace shook her head. "I have not even entered this season yet. I am only participating in soirees at my hosts' behest. How could I be settled on a gentleman when I am not truly partaking in the season?"

Her mother did not look convinced. Grace held her breath, waiting to know what her mother would do. Telling fibs to her mother was one thing – one easily done thing – but telling even the smallest untruth to her father was excessively challenging, especially if one wished for him to believe the falsehood. Her father was more astute than her mother. An explanation such as she had just given to her mother would likely be met with a...

"You had a season last year. However, that is neither here nor there for one does not have to be part of any season ever to marry. It is not as if parliament has amended the marriage act to include the necessity of a season."

And he would be right. She did not need a season to tell her where she hoped her heart lay. And that was precisely why she needed her mother to not get her father. None of her family needed to know that her heart was quite likely more attached to a gentleman than Felicity's would ever be. The thought of Mr. Blakesley preferring Felicity was an annoying thought to Grace at the start of her scheme. However, at this very moment, such a thought caused her heart to ache and tears to gather.

"I wish to hear naught else about him," her mother demanded.

"I cannot not speak about a friend. He calls on my hosts. I must be allowed to speak about him."

Her mother's eyes narrowed. "There will be no sighing over him or talk about being his wife."

Grace's brow furrowed. How was she going to dissuade her mother from pushing her at Mr.

Blakesley if she did not have Mr. Norman to play his part in pretending to court her?

"But what if I find I truly do wish to be his wife. It is possible."

"You will not. It is not allowed."

"You cannot decree where a heart will find its desire," Grace argued.

"I believe I just did," her mother replied in that tone which said that to say anything other than "Yes, Mother" would be met with some sort of punishment.

"Yes, Mother," Grace dutifully replied. "I will do my best not to sigh over Mr. Norman or think of him as a suitor, though he will be greatly disappointed, and I do so hate to be the cause of disappointment. It is too bad there are no convents to which I could be sent for I fear if disappointing gentlemen is to be part of gaining a husband, I am not sure I wish to find a husband."

Her mother huffed. "Do not be dramatic, Grace. Dramatics are your sister's domain."

"It is true, though. I do not like being a disappointment."

"Then, do not set your cap at Mr. Norman and

consider Mr. Blakesley instead, and you shall not disappoint me."

"Mr. Blakesley is not free," Grace protested.

"He does not appear very attached to his lady. He has done a great deal of watching you."

"Mother," Grace scolded.

"Just be polite and charming and allow him to chose for himself. I am not asking that you fling yourself at him."

"I will be his friend. I will not do more."

Her mother's smile was self-satisfied. "That should suffice."

And with that, she left Grace sitting alone on her bench until a lady, who had been standing behind them, took the seat vacated by Grace's mother.

"I did not know Mr. Blakesley had a lady," Grace's new bench mate said. "Indeed, I have never seen him with any lady in particular in all the time I have been in Bath."

"Oh, she is not from Bath." Grace's stomach twisted at the idea of spreading gossip about Walter.

"I do not see how she could not be. I do not believe Mr. Blakesley has been gone from Bath for these past six months." She leaned a bit closer to Grace. "Not even at Christmas time. His parents came here." She clucked her tongue. "If he has told you he has a lady somewhere other than in Bath, he has not been honest with you." She sighed. "And I find it difficult to believe he would be so deceptive."

Grace turned startled eyes toward her companion who seemed to know Walter quite well.

"Mrs. King," the lady said by way of introduction and then waited for Grace to introduce herself before continuing. "Mr. Blakesley helped me find a home in Bath last summer, and he introduced me to Mr. Norman, who has taken prodigiously good care of me." She patted Grace's knee. "You would not go wrong setting your cap at such a fine fellow. Mr. Blakesley and I are good friends. He visits me at least once a week." Again, she leaned close to Grace and said softly. "I suspect it is for my cook's apple cake, but I like to think it is my company which brings him to my door."

"Oh, I am sure it is your company. He would never be so crass as to visit you only for sweets," Grace rushed to assure the lady at her side.

Mrs. King laughed lightly. "Which, Miss Grace,

is precisely why he cannot have a lady anywhere but in Bath."

"Could he not have met someone here and kept up a correspondence?"

"It is possible, but I do think I would have heard about her."

Grace did not know how to respond to such a thing. "Have you met my friends?" Changing the topic of conversation would likely be a good thing.

Mrs. King looked past her to where Bea sat. "No, I have not."

"Mrs. King, this is Mrs. Clayton. She is my cousin with whom I am staying. Her husband, who is next to her, is a friend of Mr. Blakesley. Bea, this is Mrs. King, whom I have just met."

"Ah!" Mrs. King clapped her hands in delight. "You have leased Erondale, have you not?"

"Yes," Bea replied.

"And have you found it to your liking?"

"Very much so."

"I have heard about you. Such a lovely man Mr. Blakesley is." She leaned close to Grace. "You'd not go wrong setting your cap at him. Your mother is not wrong about that."

"Mr. and Mrs. Shelton are also staying at Erondale," Grace added, for she did not know what else to say. "They are currently dancing."

"As is my niece. See her there – in the light blue with Mr. Baily — the short blond gentleman?"

Grace turned her eyes toward the dancers and sought out a lady in light blue who was dancing with a short fellow. It took a minute or two as the partners were separated and then reunited by the dance.

"She is very pretty." A trifle older looking than most of the ladies who were dancing. In fact, she looked at least as old as Mr. Baily.

"She has come to keep me company since she has not yet taken."

"Oh." She was a companion?

"However, I will not call her my companion," Mrs. King whispered. "Her father would, but my brother has never been good with words or a lady's feelings. He is more of a facts and figures sort of person."

Mrs. King was certainly a talkative sort of woman, but she seemed rather nice despite that fact. After all, Mr. Blakesley was her friend.

"Is your niece very old then?" Grace whispered.

"Seven and twenty."

Grace gasped.

"She is rather firmly on the shelf if I cannot find her a match." Mrs. King chuckled. "I think that is truly why her father sent her to me. I have been known to make some very good matches." She looked Grace up and down. "You really should consider Mr. Blakesley. I do believe you would suit quite nicely. As for Mr. Norman?" She shook her head. "You need someone more attentive."

"Oh, but he is attentive."

Mrs. King's brows rose. "When he is present, he is, but how often is he not present?"

Grace shrugged.

"You would grow lonely. That would never be the case with Mr. Blakesley." She winked at Grace. "Do not be afraid to consider it. I promise I will not say a word to your mother." She chuckled. "I remember when my mother was pushing me at this gentleman and that." She smoothed her skirt. "In fact, there was this one time..."

Grace could see why Walter only visited Mrs. King once a week. The woman was an excellent storyteller, and as the second song of the set began, meaning that Mrs. King's niece would not be coming to collect her any time soon, Grace had to admit that a cup of tea and a slice of apple cake would be a rather perfect complement to her story.

Chapter 14

"Are you watching my sister?"

Walter turned toward Felicity with the idea to put her off with a partially truthful answer, but he had no more than opened his mouth than her mother was answering for him.

"I dare say he is. Why would he not be?"

"Actually, I was noticing that Mrs. King has made an appearance at tonight's soiree, which means her niece must have arrived. She does not attend assemblies on her own account. She is more of a theatre or concert-going lady."

"Who is Mrs. King?" Mrs. Love inquired.

"She is the lady sitting with Miss Grace." Walter's answer earned him a pleased smile from Grace's mother. "I should go give her my greetings since we are good friends."

"Are you certain that is the reason you wish to

go over there?" There was a note of teasing in Mrs. Love's question.

"Yes." It was one reason he wished to cross the room. The other reason had to do with preferring to be with Grace rather than her sister.

"Are you engaged for the next dance?" Mrs. Love asked as Felicity batted her lashes.

"No," Walter replied, "nor do I plan to be. There is a cardroom which is, no doubt, missing my presence, although I may have to do my duty in regard to Mrs. King's niece as I did promise to dance with her at least once after her arrival. It seemed the least I could do to help the girl settle into her new surroundings." As he smiled at a somewhat affronted looking Felicity, his eye caught Grace's attention on him.

"If you will excuse me." He gave Felicity and her mother a bow and made his escape.

"I say, Blakesley," Roger said as Walter joined him and his wife, who had just completed their set, "Miss Love is looking daggers at you."

"Yes, I suppose she is."

Roger leaned toward him. "What did you do?"

"It is what I did not do," Walter replied. "I did

not ask her to dance as she and her mother seemed to wish for me to do."

"Indeed?" A pleased smirk settled on Roger's mouth. "Is that all?"

"No," Walter replied. "I also mentioned needing to do my duty in standing up with Mrs. King's niece despite my desire to find the card room."

Roger let out a low whistle.

Walter shrugged. "I do not intend on ever dancing with Miss Love."

"Is there a reason?" Mrs. Shelton asked.

Walter nodded. "The evening when I first met Miss Grace, she asked me not to dance with her sister."

Mrs. Shelton sighed just a bit as a smile lit her face.

He took two steps away from the Sheltons. "Mrs. King," he greeted.

"Mr. Blakesley. How good it is to see you! I was just beginning to despair that you might be too tangled up in willing young dance partners to see me."

"What? Never say you thought so," Walter replied in the same playful fashion in which Mrs. King's comment was made. She was wearing her teasing grin – the one she always wore when mentioning his lack of a wife and her desire to help him remedy such a blight.

"I have made a new friend in your absence." Her brows waggled at him. "She was telling me that you have a lady of whom you have not told me."

Mortification settled over Grace's features.

"Well," Walter said, "that is because it is a new arrangement."

Mrs. King's eye narrowed with suspicion.

"And I did not know until very recently how such a thing might progress. Therefore, I could not tell you about it."

Mrs. King looked slightly mollified. "I should hope you intended to tell me."

"Oh, most certainly." He would tell anyone who would listen, as soon as Grace came to trust him enough to allow him to openly court her.

"I understand she is not from Bath."

"No, she is not," Walter answered truthfully. "She is from Kent, though she is not there at present as her family is travelling." He was pleased to see amusement in Grace's eyes.

"It would be lovely if they were to come to Bath,"

Mrs. King said, giving Walter a pointed look, "so that I might meet her."

"That would be lovely," Walter agreed before adding, "I think you would like her."

"Well, if she is anything like Miss Grace, here, I know I would. I would suggest you ask my new friend to dance, but I understand you have already done so." Her lips curled up into that teasing smile again. "However there is no law or stricture saying you cannot ask Miss Grace for a second dance."

Walter chuckled and shifted his gaze to Grace. "I fear Miss Grace would not wish for me to do so, for then she would have to refuse me."

"Refuse you?" Mrs. King looked at Grace as if there was something wrong with the girl.

"Because a second dance would signify marked attention," Walter answered. He would like nothing better than to make such a declaration, but he would not push Grace beyond where she had so far willing allowed him to lead her.

"Paw, such nonsense!"

"And, if you would allow me, I should like to request a set of your niece."

Mrs. King tipped her head and lifted an eyebrow as if she thought it was not at all sensible to be refusing Grace to offer for her niece, who had just joined them.

"Thank you, Mr. Bailey." Mrs. King's niece dipped a curtsey as her partner left her with her aunt.

"Annabelle," Mrs. King began, "I would like you to meet Mr. Blakesley. Mr. Blakesley, this is my niece, Miss Annabelle Chapman."

"Miss Chapman, it is a pleasure to finally put a face to the name I have heard so many times."

"Likewise," Miss Chapman replied with a wide and welcoming smile. She did not seem the sort to be retiring or off-putting. Indeed, she was very pretty and radiated pleasantness.

"Would I be able to convince you, on such short acquaintance, to dance with me?" Walter offered.

Miss Chapman laughed softly. "I believe, Mr. Blakesley, that though we have only just met, we are likely well-acquainted. My aunt is not known for her retiring nature or for her lack of stories to share."

Mrs. King huffed and clucked her tongue before saying, "Such impertinence!" To which, Miss Chapman's only reply to her aunt was a smile.

"I would be pleased to dance with you," she said to Walter.

"Excellent," Walter answered. "Perhaps you can tell me a few stories about your aunt."

Again, Mrs. King huffed.

"Miss Grace, I must apologize for not being here earlier." Norman was straightening a sleeve as he hurried up to them. He opened his mouth to speak but snapped it shut again upon seeing Mrs. King and her niece. Oddly, his friend seemed at a loss for how to proceed. Even more odd was the fact that Mrs. King did not attempt to introduce him to her niece, and that niece seemed to be embarrassed.

Grace gave a quick glance around the group and then, said, "There is nothing to forgive. One cannot schedule emergencies around a dance card."

"Oh, indeed," Norman managed to say.

"I am free for this dance," Grace prompted.

Norman nodded. "That would be wonderful." He extended his hand to her. "Might we walk a bit before we take our places?"

Grace looked to Graeme, who nodded his consent. Then, she put her hand in Norman's and rose.

Walter watched Grace leave with his friend.

"They are all wrong for each other," Mrs. King

muttered. "And I have told Miss Grace that very thing." She took her niece's hand and winked at her when Annabelle looked her direction. "Mr. Norman, who I have taken on as my physician, requires a different sort of lady, and Miss Grace requires a different sort of gentleman."

"Mr. Norman is your physician?"

Was there a touch of horror mixed with the surprise in Miss Chapman's tone?

"Yes, Mr. Blakesley recommended him upon my settling into my house," Mrs. King replied.

"But—"

Mrs. King shook her head ever so slightly, keeping her niece from saying anything further. "Mr. Norman is excellent at his profession and well-respected."

"Then, I am happy you have found him." She turned from her aunt to Walter. "Our set will begin soon."

"Of course." Walter offered her his arm and led her onto the dance floor. "Are you well?"

Miss Chapman nodded. "It is nearly overwhelming finding one's footing in a new town."

"It can be," Walter agreed. "Have you found Bath to your liking so far?"

"Oh, yes! It is beautiful, and my aunt is delightful. We have always gotten on exceptionally well." Miss Chapman leaned a bit closer to him. "She has long been my confidant." One shoulder lifted and lowered in a shrug. "My mother has more than just me with whom to be concerned. There were six of us. Three boys, and three girls."

"Six children?" That was a sizable family.

She nodded. "I am the oldest and least likely to marry, so I have been sent to stay with my aunt."

"Least –?" Walter looked at her in shock unable to complete his question. She did not seem unmarriageable to him.

"My ideas about who would make a good husband do not mesh with those of my father," she said in explanation. "Therefore, I shall not marry."

"Oh." He took his place across from her in line.

"Father is very traditional and unyielding."

The first notes of the song began, and Walter prepared to remember his steps while attempting not to spend too much time pondering Miss Chapman's predicament. However, as it turned out, he was not the only curious person in their set who was attempting to put things together.

"I think Mr. Norman knows her," Grace whispered to Walter when the steps of the song brought them together. "He is very flustered."

Yes, Walter could see that. Usually, his friend was the picture of serenity. Not much unsettled him, which was a very good quality for a physician to have. Walter hopped from his right foot to his left foot and, taking his partner's hands, circled.

Miss Chapman smiled at him, and he returned it. She was aptly named for she was indeed a beauty – not in the strict classical sense, but in a fashion which was heightened by her smile and the sparkle in her eye – and belle did mean... He nearly faltered in his steps. Belle. This was Belle. The Belle. The lady whom Norman sought each year to replace and never found any who could take her place.

"He says she is a friend from long ago," Grace shared with him when once again they were brought together.

"A very good friend, I believe," Walter replied with a speaking look.

"Oh! Is it a tragic story?" she asked.

Walter only had time to nod before they were separated again. According to Norman, he and Belle had been immediately taken with one another. However, they were never allowed to even converse if it could be prevented. Being young and in love, they attempted at every turn to thwart the intervention of her parents and the brother who was closest to Miss Chapman in age.

It was this brother who had turned Norman away for good. A few well-placed disparaging hints regarding his ability to do his duty as a physician with any degree of skill had made it challenging for him to find a place to practice his profession, and so Norman had left his home county to make a new start of things in Bath.

"Does your brother know that Mr. Norman is your aunt's physician?" he asked when the song was over and he was leading Miss Chapman back to her aunt.

Her eyes grew wide. "You know about that?"

"Mr. Norman and I are good friends. I put the pieces together. Does he know?"

She shook her head. "My brother died."

"My condolences."

"Thank you. It was a year and a half ago now, so the shock of it is gone."

And his friend was, at least, safe from her brother's machinations. However, his friend did not know that.

"Thank you for the dance, Mr. Blakesley," Miss Chapman said as they reached her aunt.

"The pleasure was all mine," he assured her, and then made his excuses about needing to visit the card room. However, the card room was not where he was truly going. Mr. Norman had left the room, and there was an important bit of information Walter needed to share with him.

Chapter 15

"Come with me." Felicity took Grace by the arm when Grace's set of dances had ended and she and Mr. Norman were leaving the floor in the direction of the Claytons and Mrs. King.

"But Mr. Norman –"

"I have need of my sister's assistance, Mr. Norman." Felicity directed one of her most charming smiles at him. It was the one Grace had seen her use many times on various gentlemen to get her way. "You would not keep me from my sister, would you?"

"But..." Grace once again attempted to extract herself from her sister's grasp. "Bea and Mr. Clayton will be expecting me to return to them."

"Mr. Norman can relay a message." Felicity's eyelashes fluttered as her hold on her sister tightened.

She might feign innocence, but Grace knew better. There was some scheme brewing in her sister's mind, and it was most likely a scheme in which Grace did not wish to take part. Of course, that would not matter to Felicity. She rarely cared about what Grace did or did not want.

"I will inform them of your being with your sister," Mr. Norman said quickly.

It was almost as if the man wanted to run from Grace's presence, but she knew that could not be true. In fact, she suspected that it was the presence of another young lady from which Mr. Norman wished to flee, and Grace had hoped to discover somewhat more about that particular young lady. Being drawn away from her goal by her sister was most distressful.

"What do you want?" Grace demanded as Mr. Norman scurried over to the Claytons. "I have friends with whom I wish to sit."

"I do not know why you are so disagreeable," Felicity said as she drew Grace toward the door. "You have been barely civil to me since you went to stay with the Claytons. I am not certain they are the best friends to have if they are going to make you so prickly."

Grace drew a calming breath through her nose

and released it. "Have you ever considered that it is not the influence of my hosts but rather your behaviour which makes me cross?"

"My behaviour?" Felicity questioned with some surprise. "I do not see how I could be the cause of your foul humor."

"You seriously do not see how?"

"Do keep your voice down, Grace," Felicity scolded. "Yes, I do not see how I could be the cause."

Grace knew in these sorts of moments when her displeasure was stirred as it was now that, unless she could bite her tongue hard enough to keep it from wagging, she should turn and walk away. However, what she knew and what she did were not of the same level of wisdom. Frustration at her sister's behaviour bubbled over as Grace straightened her gloves while attempting to keep her composure. It was the sight of her well-stitched and pretty repair to Felicity's gloves which overruled her good sense. She drew her sister into the corridor and toward the vestibule of the Assembly rooms instead of allowing herself to be steered to the tearoom.

"Have you no recollection of Mr. Everett Clayton?" Grace hissed as they stepped to the side to avoid walking into a cluster of people.

"Of course, I remember him," Felicity said. "I truly cared for him."

"Cared for him?" Grace parroted with no little amount of astonishment. "You flaunted Mr. Ramsey in front of the poor man."

"I did not flaunt Mr. Ramsey."

Grace rolled her eyes and shook her head. Her sister was completely lost to all good sense if she could not see such a thing!

"You flaunted. Most distastefully," Grace retorted. "Do you know why I am wearing these gloves?" Grace thrust her hand in front of her sister's face.

"Because gloves are the thing."

"No, because you could not be bothered to repair these, so you cast them aside to your poor sister who did not need them since she was not to have a season. And do you know why your unfortunate sister was not to have a season?" She waited for a full half-second for Felicity to respond before answering in her stead. "Because you flaunted Mr. Ramsey and deserted Mr. Clayton, and now, you are in danger of never being wed if your season is not successful and Mr. Ramsey is led along and then rejected just as Mr. Clayton was."

Felicity's mouth, which had gaped during Grace's diatribe, snapped shut. "I wished to tell you that I think Mr. Ramsey is going to offer for me tomorrow. He has just asked if he could call on me privately, and Father agreed."

"Oh." That was not what Grace had expected to hear.

"I love him, Grace."

Grace's brow furrowed.

"I know I thought I loved Mr. Clayton, but this time is different."

"How so? Is it because he has a larger estate?"

Her sister shrugged. "I will not deny that his estate is an inducement to think well of him, although it is not as prosperous as it should be, and my dowry will be needed to make any improvements I should desire."

"He wishes to marry you for your money?"

Felicity shook her head. "He is not a fortune hunter, for he has been honest with me about the state of his finances. He has even discussed them with Father and taken notes on the advice Father has given him. He loves me, and I love him."

Grace was not certain her sister knew what love was. "If his estate were to be taken from him, would you still wish to marry him?"

"Yes."

"If he was told he had to chose between his estate – his future inheritance which would provide for him and his family for generations to come – and marrying you, would you let him choose you to his detriment?"

"Why would I not?" Confusion etched a furrow between her eyebrows.

"You would allow him to do that which would harm him? Do you not care for his happiness?"

"Of course, I care for his happiness, and I know he would not be happy without me. He has said so many times."

Grace was not convinced. "What if you did not have a sizable dowry? Would he still have chosen you?"

Felicity blinked. "I do not know for certain, but I believe he would have."

"Ask him."

The suggestion was met with rolling eyes.

"I would want to know," Grace added in explanation.

"Do you not trust him?"

"I trust very few." She trusted Bea and Mr. Clayton, as well as Mr. and Mrs. Shelton, and of course, Mr. Norman and – she nearly sighed – Walter. Perhaps it was more accurate to say she trusted all save her sister and anyone who appeared to love her sister. However, that would be rather rude to say, though the thought was tempting.

"No, you trust everyone," Felicity countered. "You always have."

Grace shook her head. "Not any longer."

"What do you mean?"

"I trusted you. I helped you win Mr. Everett Clayton from Bea when we both knew she liked him. Not that she was the only one who admired him. I told you that I did, do you remember that? And what did you tell me?"

"That I was the oldest and should marry first."

Grace nodded. "So, I trusted your wisdom and allowed you to pursue Mr. Everett Clayton. No, that is not entirely true, I helped you pursue him. My heart was not attached, but you claimed yours was." Her lips pursed in displeasure. "As it turns out your attachment was less than mine."

They had nearly reached the portico and stood

just where they could see the entrances for those arriving in carriages. A few people were strolling along the corridors but one couple was not strolling and was instead standing very close to each other. The gentleman looked rather familiar to Grace.

"I thought I was firmly attached to him. Truly, I did," Felicity was saying just as the gentleman Grace was watching turned enough for her to see his face.

She sucked in a quick breath. "We should return to the ballroom. Mother will worry." She turned her sister toward the interior of the building.

"I do not believe we have concluded this discussion," Felicity protested. "I have not finished pleading my case."

"You cannot convince me of that which I do not wish to be convinced," Grace retorted.

Felicity pulled away from Grace. "Why do you keep looking down that corridor."

"For no reason," Grace lied as she attempted to turn her sister back toward the interior of the building, but to no avail.

"I love Mr. Blakesley," she blurted.

That arrested her sister's motions and spun her around.

"Mr. Blakesley? Truly? Not Mr. Norman?"

"I do not love Mr. Norman. I love Mr. Blakesley – or I am almost certain I do." Her heart raced. On the list of all the people who were not to know about Mr. Blakesley, her sister sat at the top. She should not have made such an admission, but she also could not allow her sister to see Mr. Ramsey with whomever it was that had her hands on the gentleman's jacket, straightening the buttons. As much as she did not trust her sister and was excessively unhappy with her for the way she had treated Mr. Everett Clayton, she could not bring herself to knowingly allow her sister to be harmed and humiliated publicly. Oh, she knew some would disagree with her – Roger, for one – but she was just not able to knowingly cause harm to her sister.

Her hand flew to her heart. He was right. Walter was right. She did have a caring heart. She needed to find him and tell him that their charade could come to an end. If he was right about her having a caring heart, he was likely also right about not needing to trust her sister but to only trust him.

"What did Mr. Blakesley talk to you about earlier tonight?" Grace asked.

Felicity blinked. "I will tell you if you will tell me why you have been playing with Mr. Norman's affections." She crossed her arms and scowled at Grace. "And all the while you were berating me for how I treated Mr. Everett Clayton, you have been doing no better."

Grace huffed as she pushed her sister forward and deeper into the building. "About what did you talk to Mr. Blakesley?"

"I attempted to get him to ask me to dance – after I teased him about watching you, that is." She sighed. "He refused."

"He did?" Grace smiled. Oh, she had been such a fool to think Walter was the sort to fall for her sister's charming manners. Of course, he was not the sort! He was not like any other gentleman she had met.

"Oh, he made it very clear that he did not wish to dance with me."

The bitter edge to Felicity's tone made Grace smile just a bit more broadly.

"Mother will be delighted to hear she does not need to worry about Mr. Norman."

Grace gasped. "No! You must not tell her. Not yet."

"Why ever not?"

"I have to tell Walter first."

Felicity's eyes grew wide. "Walter? Has he given you leave to call him by his Christian name?"

She would have to give herself a very stern lecture later about thinking before speaking. "Yes, but only in private."

"Oh," her sister cried eagerly, "there is so much you must tell me."

"No, there is not. I have told you all I am going to tell you."

"I am afraid, dear sister, that, if you do not wish for me to tell Mother about your declaration, there is more you must share with me."

Grace closed her eyes and sighed. She should have known Felicity would dangle that in front of her. Felicity was, after all, very adept at getting what she wanted.

"Very well, I will tell you a bit more, but not right now. I must speak to Mr. Blakesley first."

"I believe Mother wished to call at Erondale tomorrow, perhaps I will join her."

"What about Mr. Ramsey's private call?"

Her sister's lips pursed with displeasure while Grace felt rather smug for having thwarted Felicity's plan. Of course, there might not be a need for a private conversation between Felicity and Mr. Ramsey once Mr. Ramsey's duplicity was revealed — later. Much later. Not here. Not now. For here and now, she would pretend that she had not seen what she saw.

Chapter 16

Walter took a turn of the cardroom before proceeding out of it and toward the entryway. Ahead of him, Grace seemed to be pulling her sister along, and from the expression on Grace's face, it was not because she was excited to show something of interest to her sister. It looked very much as if Grace was excessively put out with Felicity.

Despite the tantalizing intrigue posed by Grace and her sister, he ducked into the tearoom to see if his friend was there.

As fortune would have it, he was. Norman was sitting at a far table, doing his best not to be pulled into any conversation.

Norman glanced up as Walter joined him. "I cannot leave Bath. I will not. However, I must find someone to recommend to Mrs. King in my stead."

"I do not think you need to do either."

Norman leaned forward. "Her niece is Belle."

Walter nodded. "I know. I figured that out."

"Then, you know precisely why I must not continue my care of Mrs. King."

"No, I do not know."

Was Norman actually glowering at him? This was not the calm, rarely-ruffled-until-Walter-had-pushed-him-too-far friend with whom Walter was acquainted. But then, loss of love and having that loss tossed in front of a gentleman unawares would likely have an unnerving effect on anyone.

"Miss Chapman is lovely."

"I know." The words rumbled from his friend, causing Walter's eyebrows to lift.

"We had a very pleasant, if short and somewhat halting, discussion during our dance."

The comment was met with a small huff and narrowed eyes.

"It seems her family is not so large as it used to be."

There. Surprise and curiosity. Those were much more welcome expressions on Norman's face.

"A certain brother died."

Norman blinked. "Died?"

Walter nodded. "I believe she said it was a bit

more than a year ago, and from the sounds of things, it was sudden."

"It matters not. Her father will still not approve of someone like me. Was it an accident?"

Walter shrugged. "I did not ask. My apologies."

Norman shook his head. "I do not need to know. It changes nothing."

"She is seven and twenty. She does not need her father's approval." He held Norman's gaze and watched his friend wilt from anger to sadness.

"I cannot."

"Why?"

"It would create a gulf between her and her family. I cannot do that."

"You do not know that." Walter held up a hand to stop Norman's protest. "You think you know that, but until you talk to the lady, you cannot know that."

"I am not you, Blakesley."

"And a good thing that is. I am not sure that Bath could survive as well as it does without your unique ability to care for one and all."

"You care for people, too. Do not even attempt to tell me that you do not have a fondness for half the people in Bath. How many of them know you by name and sing your praises?"

"Nearly as many as know and praise you."

"That is not the point," Norman protested.

"I believe it is."

Norman pushed up from his seat. "Miss Grace, Miss Love, is all well?"

"Perfectly well." Miss Love's eyes seemed to be dancing with merriment. Walter was uncertain if that was a good thing or as dreadful as he imagined it might be. "I believe my sister was looking for you, Mr. Blakesley."

Grace's eyes closed, and she shook her head but only just. Did she not wish to see him?

"Then, she is in luck as you have found me – not that I was hiding, of course." He rose and offered a chair to Miss Love.

"No, no. I will sit beside Mr. Norman."

There was a gleefulness to the comment that unsettled him.

"I was on my way to see Mr. and Mrs. Clayton." Grace looked pointedly at her sister while Walter helped her with her chair.

"And we are still on our way, but there is that bit of information I so wish to know."

"I am not telling you here."

"Oh, well, of course not. We would take a turn of the corridor."

"I meant here in this building."

It seemed as if Grace was still put out by her sister.

"We could all take a stroll," Felicity suggested.

"No!" Grace snapped.

"I would not be opposed to it," Walter said softly.

"I would be."

"You would?" Did she need to be so adamant in her attempt to make it appear as if she cared for no one but Norman?

"Yes, I would. I should like very much to be returned to my party."

"I will not detain you." If she was in such a hurry to be away from him, then he was not going to stop her.

She melted a bit, her shoulders slumping forward while her head drooped.

"It is not that I do not wish to speak with you. It is just that I do not wish for my cousin to worry."

The corner of her lower lip was drawn between her teeth. Something was not right with her.

Walter stood. "I insist. I am in need of some air, and do not wish to escort myself."

She turned wide eyes to him and shook her head ever so slightly.

"If you will not accompany me, then perhaps your sister would?" He smiled at Felicity.

"If I must." Felicity batted her lashes, but not at him. The expression was directed at her sister.

"Oh, very well." Grace stood. "I will accompany Mr. Blakesley for a short stroll of the corridor. However, I am still not telling you anything tonight," she added to her sister.

Miss Love did not look as if she believed what Grace had said, but she was delighted when Walter offered Grace his arm and it was accepted.

"I will be right here with Mr. Norman," Felicity said as they were leaving the table.

"I would rather that she would go back to my mother," Grace grumbled.

"I take it you are displeased with your sister?"

"Not as much as I am with myself and Mr. Ramsey."

That was not the response he had expected. But then, Grace was a rather interesting and surprising young woman. "What have you and Mr. Ramsey done?"

"I saw Mr. Ramsey with some lady down the passage that leads to the carriages, and so I told my sister I love you. I could not let her see Mr. Ramsey, after all."

Walter stopped walking. "I am not certain I heard that correctly."

"Mr. Ramsey was down there –" She waved her hand toward the carriage entrance.

"Not that part," Walter stopped her. "Though I am curious about that. You love me?"

"Yes, and my sister knows. Therefore, our scheme is at an end, for I am certain she is incapable of keeping such a thing hidden from my mother and once my mother knows..." She sighed. "Everyone will know."

"And why is this a problem?" Her lip was between her teeth again and her eyes were lowered.

"I will not have you all to myself."

He had to lean towards her to hear what she said.

"I do not wish to have our secret discovered. It is so lovely and private when just we and a few others knew."

"Do you still fear that I will fall prey to your sister's charms?" Was that the real reason why she did not wish to have others know?

She shook her head. "You did not dance with her tonight. She said she attempted to get you to ask her."

"Of course, I did not dance with her. You asked me not to," he replied. Why could she not have declared her love for him when they were at his townhouse playing billiards? Why did it have to be in a busy corridor at the Upper Rooms?

"I did?"

He nodded. "When we first met and you refused to dance with me in favor of dancing with Norman."

She blinked. "I did, did I not?"

"Yes, and I do not break my promises."

"But you did not promise me that you would not dance with her." Her brow was furrowed.

"Did I not nod and smile at you when you were lining up with Mr. Norman?"

Her lips pursed as she thought. "You did!"

"That was my promise," he said. "And I will never break a promise I have made to you. Even if I found your sister charming – which I do not — I would not break it."

How he wanted to take her in his arms. She was wearing that compelling look of longing she had worn the day he had traced her silhouette at Erondale.

"Now, about Mr. Ramsey." A change of subject might make things a trifle easier. Or so he hoped.

"You really do not find Felicity charming?"

Walter shook his head.

Her lashes fluttered as delight overtook her features. "That may be the thing I love most about you, Mr. Blakesley."

"About Mr. Ramsey," Walter tried again. As much as he wished to stand here and discuss her love for him, here was not a safe place to do so. For such a conversation would make it a great deal more challenging to not kiss her, and, as it was, he was struggling with wanting to do just that.

"He was in the corridor with a lady. They were standing very close – closer than we are – and her hands were on his jacket." She glanced to her right and then back at him. "If we were in the garden at Erondale, I would show you."

He was beginning to understand why Grace was so despondent about their scheme being found out. It would be likely that such secret and intimate moments would be a thing of the past for some time – at least until he could marry her.

"I do not know who that lady was. I have never seen her at any of the soirees I have attended, but then, I have not attended very many."

"I should speak to your father."

"About Mr. Ramsey?"

Walter shook his head. "I apologize. I was thinking about being alone in the garden with you and not fully attending to what you were saying."

Her smile was enchanting. The sooner he spoke to her father the better.

"We should likely take you back and save Mr. Norman from your sister, and then, I will take a roam around the place and see if I can find out anything about Mr. Ramsey and his mysterious lady."

"Will you?"

"For you, I will." He barely refrained from lifting her fingers to his lips.

"Oh, Miss Grace."

Walter turned to find Mrs. King approaching them.

"What a delight to find you here and with Mr. Blakesley." There was that teasing note to her voice once again. "Annabelle and I were just getting some air and contemplating going home."

"So soon?" Grace asked.

"It seems the evening has lost its sheen."

"That is unfortunate."

"Indeed, it is, Mr. Blakesley. I have not even had the opportunity to question you about your secret courtship with some lady from – where was she from?"

"She is from Kent," Walter answered. "My secret angel is from Kent. And," he added, "now that I am at liberty to do so, I will tell you all about her some-day when I call."

"I should hope you will. I had not thought you so secretive."

"Normally, I am not. However, the young lady asked me to be, and I can deny her nothing."

Mrs. King tilted her head and smiled at him as a proud mother might gaze upon a child who had done something of merit.

"Now, see, Miss Grace, this is why I thought you should set your cap at him instead of Mr. Norman." She shrugged. "But, it seems you were correct, and he is not free."

No, he was not free. His heart was irrevocably gone both now and forever.

"I still would not have you set your cap at Mr. Norman," Mrs. King was instructing Grace as Miss Chapman looked ill beside her aunt.

"I do not plan to," Grace assured her, and Miss Chapman expelled a breath as if she was relieved.

It seemed there was a great deal of hope for Norman to finally gain the lady as his own — if Norman could be made to see reason, that is.

"I believe we would be more than delighted to have you call on us, Miss Grace. My Annabelle is in need of some good friends."

"I would like nothing better."

Walter could hear the excitement in Grace's voice and knew that she was more than delighted by the idea of calling on Mrs. King and her niece. "We could call together," he suggested. "If your cousin would join us, that is, Miss Grace."

Mrs. King's head pulled back in surprise. "But would that not make your lady uneasy to hear you are making calls with a lady as pretty as Miss Grace?"

"I think she could tolerate it."

Mrs. King did not look convinced. Therefore,

after he had excused himself to see Grace back to her party but before he had actually removed himself completely from Mrs. King's presence, he leaned near her ear as he passed her and whispered, "Miss Grace is from Kent."

Chapter 17

"Grace. Grace. You must wake up."

Was that her mother? Grace popped one eye open just far enough to see her mother sitting on the side of the bed with Bea standing in her robe behind her.

Grace yawned. "What time is it?" Had she slept until calling hours? Last night had been tiring in a wonderful sort of way so it was possible that she had slept far longer than was her normal wont, though she did feel a great deal more tired than she would expect to feel if it was late enough for calling hours.

"It is six o'clock," Bea answered.

No, she had not slept late. It was indeed as early as it felt. She closed her eyes.

"Why are you here, Mama?"

"Something has happened. It is most dreadful. I

do not know how I have managed not to succumb to the horror of it, but I knew I must get you before I could think about myself."

Drowsiness fled and Grace propped herself up on her elbows. "What has happened? Is someone ill?"

"We must go home immediately."

Grace sat up. Her heart was racing. "Why? What has happened? Tell me what has happened."

Mrs. Love wrung her hands together – which Grace noticed were not gloved. Her mother never left her house without a pair of gloves on her hands. Something was most certainly wrong.

"Mr. Ramsey has..." She leaned toward Grace and lowered her voice. "He has quit Bath and abandoned your sister."

No! He could not have. She could not believe it. Not after what Felicity had told her. "But he asked Father to speak to Felicity in private."

"Yes, yes, he did. We were all so certain he was going to make her an offer, but then..." She covered her mouth with her hand and shook her head. "When we arrived home from the ball, there was a note awaiting us which said he would not be able to call tomorrow. Well, Felicity wished to know why, as is natural — I am sure I wished to know, too — so, your sister sent a note to him asking for his reason. However, no reply was forthcoming. The messenger was told that the master was not available to give a reply. Your father and I figured it was because of the lateness of the hour, and we would discover what we needed to know on the morrow." She rose from her perch on the bed. "Your sister was not satisfied, and after we all went to bed, she... Oh, it is too dreadful."

"May I get you a glass of wine?" Bea offered as she led Mrs. Love to a chair.

"No, no. I will be well as soon as we are gone from this dreadful place. I shall never wish to see Bath again. Oh, what are we to do?"

"Shall I call for your husband?" Bea asked.

Mrs. Love shook her head. "It is a mother's job to speak of these things."

Grace was out of bed and kneeling beside her mother. "You are frightening me, Mama. Please, tell me what has happened. What did Felicity do?"

"You know how impatient your sister can be."

Yes, Grace was well aware of Felicity's desire to have or know things immediately.

"Oh, she is ruined!" Mrs. Love cried.

"How is she ruined?" Grace begged. Her mother could be so trying at times!

"She went to the rooms he is renting."

Was Felicity mad?

"By herself?" Grace asked.

Her mother nodded.

Of all the stupid things to do!

"In the middle of the night?" Grace asked.

Again, her mother nodded. "It seems it was not the first time she has done so."

Dread settled around Grace's heart. She was all too familiar with her sister's propensity to sneak away and behave inappropriately. "Where is she now?"

"Downstairs with your father and Mr. Clayton."

That was a relief. Had Felicity been left to her own devices, she might have attempted to follow Mr. Ramsey.

"And where is Mr. Ramsey?" Bea asked before Grace could.

"No one knows. He has not returned to his rooms."

"But his things, Mama." Grace grasped her mother's hand attempting to capture her mother's quickly deteriorating attention. "He will have to return for his things or have them sent. Surely, someone will soon know where he is. We only need to wait and be patient. He could be anywhere doing anything. We do not know that he has quit Bath."

"But he has! He has quit Bath, for that is what Felicity was told when she inquired of the gentleman who keeps the room below Mr. Ramsey's."

"She spoke to someone?" Oh, that was not good. Sneaking in and out was always best done when no one discovered the activity.

Mrs. Love nodded as tears began to spill down her cheeks. "She may be with child."

Grace's stomach attempted to tie itself in a knot. How could Felicity do such a thing as that? Kissing a gentleman was one thing but to allow him to bed her? Oh, it was unthinkable!

"Do you know this for certain?" Bea asked.

"Her father quizzed her most thoroughly. It is a very real possibility."

"Then, it is imperative that we remain in Bath until we discover where Mr. Ramsey has gone." He must be made to marry her, if not for her sister's sake, at least, for the sake of the child. If her stomach was not so knotted, Grace was nearly certain she would have cast up her accounts at the thought of such wickedness as a gentleman abandoning a lady, whom he claimed to love and had seduced, as well as his child.

"He quit Bath with another lady. He has used your sister very ill."

The image of the lady in the corridor at the Upper Rooms sprang to mind. "Oh, dear. Did this lady have blond hair?"

"I really do not know. Why do you ask such a thing?"

"Because I saw him with some blond-haired lady last night at the assembly in the passageway to the carriages. They looked very cozy, and I thought it strange. I was going to tell you about it tomorrow – I mean today – before Felicity had her private interview with Mr. Ramsey." She was not about to allow her sister to accept such a fellow without telling her of what had been seen, and she had hoped to know more about who the lady was once Walter called on her this morning.

"It is too late now. Your father insists that you prepare to depart as soon as can be. We cannot stay here any longer. The shame is too much. It shall surely taint you as well."

"But I did nothing wrong!" Grace cried.

"That may be, but to be the sister of such a wanton woman! Oh, you are ruined."

Grace sat backwards on the floor. "No, no. I will not leave."

"You have no choice in this matter. If we can leave quietly and find a place for your sister..." Her mother's voice trailed off as she began to weep.

"I will help you," Bea offered. "As soon as I see that your mother has been safely returned to your father."

"I cannot leave."

"It is best," Bea said. "The less gossip there is, the better."

No! No, it was not best. She could not and would not leave Walter. How could her mother ask her to give up her happiness because of her sister? True, her mother did not know about her attachment to Mr. Blakesley, but that did not matter. It was still horribly unfair to be asked to leave Bath and her friends just because her sister was stupid.

"Oh, what gentleman would want to be tied to such a family? We are doomed," her mother wailed.

Her mother's words fell heavily on Grace. Would being married to her cause Walter harm?

Would his business endeavors suffer? Would she be shunned by his family? And would that, in turn, bring even more misery to him?

As Bea helped Mrs. Love from the room, question upon dreadful question tumbled and tangled in Grace's mind, and her heart crumbled into a thousand jagged pieces as she realized what she must do because she loved him. She could not ask him to face a life of unhappiness because of her. It was too selfish by half.

A cold deeper than the dampest, most frigid winter's day settled over her as she rose from the floor and sought a piece of paper and a pen. It was best to dissolve their scheme and end their relationship while it still remained a secret.

We have been called home unexpectedly, she wrote and paused.

No, that would not do. She tore that part of the paper off and began again.

Thank you for indulging me in my scheme and being my secret beau. I have had the most delightful time and shall cherish my memories of you. Please know that my heart shall never forget you. I wish you well and a life of happiness.

Forever your secret angel.

G-

She wiped tears from her cheek with the sleeve of her nightgown. Then, she folded the missive and wrote Mr. *Walter Blakesley* on the front before sealing it and leaving it on the desk. If Bea did not see that it was given to Mr. Blakesley, he would find it when he came to check on his house after the Claytons and Sheltons had left.

She imagined him sitting at the desk, reading her words, and smiling fondly as he remembered her. Would he find another angel? How could he not? He was handsome and had a fortune. Added to that, he was amiable and sweet. He was perfect. Absolutely, utterly perfect. Any lady would be an utter fool not to fall in love with him.

She sank down onto the bed and wiped away more tears with her sleeve.

What would his new lady be like? Who would share this house with him? Would they have loads of children or just two? Each new and troubling contemplation tore the pieces of her heart into smaller and smaller bits, leaving a vast and painful void where her heart had once been.

"Your mother is safe at your father's side. My husband has seen to getting her some wine."

Grace drew in a deep breath and released it before turning toward Bea and beginning the chore of packing.

Half an hour later, with help from Bea and her maid, Grace was appropriately dressed for travel and her trunk was ready to be tied to the carriage which would travel ahead of them to Kent.

"You did not mean to leave without a proper goodbye, did you?" Roger stood in the entry with his wife at his side. "Victoria is going to miss Philomena almost as much as she will miss you." He scratched behind Philomena's ear and then grasped Grace's hand firmly and lifted it to his lips. "Your absence will be felt by many."

Grace glanced at her mother and then leaning forward whispered. "I left him a note in my room." She simply could not leave it to chance that Walter got her message.

"I will see that it is taken care of," Roger assured her. "I wish you could stay, and I know I am not alone in such sentiments."

"No, you are not," she agreed. She wished with every fiber of her being that she could remain right her with her friends, where Walter would find her.

Victoria embraced her warmly and muttered her

sorrow at having to part and then added that she would write faithfully. Bea did the same, and then Graeme saw them all to their carriage and, after handing Philomena to Grace, gave her his wishes for a safe journey.

"You are certain he is not returning to Bath?" Grace whispered as they pulled away from Erondale. The agony in her soul deepened with each turn of the wheel down the drive.

"I think we are," her father answered.

"Could we not chase after him?"

"Chase him to where? We do not know where he has gone. And, there is no need to draw undue attention to a situation which might otherwise be dispelled of quietly."

"Felicity could have gone home, and I could have just said she was ill." She sighed as Erondale was no longer visible through the carriage window.

"I know this is not easy for you," her father replied. "You have endured a great deal."

"Far more than you know," Grace muttered. Thankfully, Felicity seemed too distraught to be a danger in revealing what she knew about Mr. Blakesley. With any luck, the strain of her current ordeal would wipe the memory of Mr. Blakesley from Felicity's mind. It was best if that part of Grace's stay in Bath remained secret.

"Come sit with me," her father said. "Your mother can sit with Felicity."

The exchange was made, and Mr. Love wrapped an arm around his youngest daughter's shoulders, kissing her forehead, and muttering his sorrow for what she must suffer. Grace snuggled into her father's side, and while stroking Philomena's fur, allowed her tears to fall unfettered, for once again, though she had not charmed him away, her sister had stolen a gentleman from Grace. Only this time, in doing so, Felicity had not crushed a gentleman's heart, but that of her own sister.

Chapter 18

Walter rubbed his neck. Sleeping on a rug on the ground even for a few hours was bound to make a gentleman stiff and sore, or, at least, that is how it was for him. The sun, which was just beginning to climb above the horizon and wake the world, was starting to warm him some as he started down the road towards home. That small amount of warmth would have to suffice until he got home and could climb into a steaming bath.

His stomach rumbled. He should have brought more food with him. However, he had not expected to be out all night trying to discover where Ramsey and his companion had gone. He had followed them to a tavern ten miles back, but from there, he could not find their trail anywhere. Who Ramsey's mystery lady was remained a mystery. No one seemed able to identify her. Of course, most of the men in the tavern had not been completely sober, and the barmaids had been too interested in flirting with him to tell him anything about some lady whom they considered a rival.

He would have to present himself empty-handed to Grace, and that fact did not sit well with him. He had promised to discover what he could, and he had done exactly that. Yet, the fact that all he could discover was nothing did not seem a fitting way to keep such a promise. Grace would want to know more. She was a curious, caring sort. In his opinion, she owed her sister little, but Grace's heart would not see it that way. No matter how much she disagreed with or disapproved of her sister, Grace would do what she could to protect her sister from harm.

He chuckled, causing his horse's ears to twitch in his direction.

"I was just thinking about your new mistress," he said to his horse. "She is a unique lady."

The horse blew a breath through its lips.

"I tell you she is. You will understand once you meet her."

Maybe today she would allow him to take her for a drive now that she was willing to reveal their secret relationship. Today, he would begin court-ing Miss Grace Love publicly, and next week, he would speak to her father. Well, he would speak to her father next week if he could be patient enough to wait until then.

His failure to obtain the information Grace sought was a small cloud on his very happy future. If he were not so stiff and sore from spending a few hours sleeping beside the road, and if his boots did not smell like the ale which an inebriated patron at that tavern had managed to spill on them, he would drive directly to Erondale. But as he was, going home to make himself presentable was the best option.

Tomorrow, he would attempt to take her with him when he called on Mrs. King, and together, they could decide how best to encourage Norman and Miss Chapmen to re-establish their friendship. Grace would likely find that to be an amusing scheme.

Again, he chuckled.

His horse blew through its lips in response.

"You are excessively cranky today, Lady," Walter called forward. "I promise you will get a good meal before we visit Miss Grace. That should set you up to be properly friendly, but if it does not, it is no matter. Miss Grace will charm you into a better mood."

From the replying snort, his horse did not seem to agree with his master's assessment, but then, Lady had not met Grace. If she had, then she'd know it to be true. Grace was ebullient. Her smile sparkled, and her eyes twinkled. Joy seemed to bubble just beneath the surface on most occasions. Even when she was repressing her enthusiasm for life and adventures, her joy seemed to need to find its release in small sighs.

And all that exuberance was soon to be his – as soon as he could talk to her father and then make his offer to her. How fortunate could one gentleman be?

~*~*~

"You seem exceptionally cheerful," Norman said to him later as Walter poured his friend a cup of tea.

"Do you wish for some?" Walter sliced a Sally Lunn in half.

"Just a quarter," Norman replied.

How the man survived on such scant meals was

beyond Walter's ability to comprehend. "Do your patients feed you?" That was likely it.

"On occasion."

"And did you see many patients this morning?"

"Two. Both with excellent cooks." Norman smiled over the rim of his cup.

Ah, so that was it. The man only ate small bits at every stop so that he could indulge in all that was offered. It was a good way of doing things. Many of the elderly women upon whom Norman called would likely find it an offense if their hospitality was refused. Mrs. King was that way.

"Did you call on Mrs. King?"

Norman shook his head. "No. Nor do I plan to call on her. I have sent a note withdrawing my services."

"You have done what?" Walter lowered his cup without taking a sip. "Have you lost all sense?"

"It would be folly for me to continue," Norman snapped.

The man was testy!

"Do you love her? And I do not mean Mrs. King." Walter finally took a sip of his tea while waiting for Norman to slowly chew a bit of his bun.

"I never stopped loving Belle, which is why I cannot pursue her."

Walter said nothing in response. Not that he did not wish to say something. He very much wanted to say several somethings, but he was not the sort to pontificate over his friend. The heart was a delicate organ. It was capable of great things such as holding onto love for an entire lifetime, but it was also easily damaged and difficult to repair when love was unrequited or worse — stolen.

"I would speak to her," was the only comment Walter allowed himself to share.

Norman simply shook his head and tore another bite off his bun.

"Mrs. King knows about Grace."

Norman looked at Walter in surprise. "How?"

"I told her – not in so many words, but I hinted quite blatantly."

"When? Did you do this last night?"

Walter nodded. "When Grace and I were taking a turn of the corridor, she and her niece found us." Walter smiled at the memory. "She loves me."

"Miss Grace?"

Once again, Walter nodded. "She told me last night." He expelled a great sigh. "I am planning to speak to her father soon. I realize we have not been acquainted long, but I see no need to wait." Not when his heart was so irrevocably lost to Grace.

"Indeed? That is excellent news!"

"Miss Chapman seemed relieved to know that Grace was not pursuing you in earnest." Walter shrugged when Norman looked at him skeptically. "You know Mrs. King and her opinions on who should be matched with whom."

Norman chuckled.

Mrs. King was excessively interested in the lives of young lovers. How many times had she suggested ladies to him only to be disappointed in his assessment that whichever lady was presented was not up to his standards? She had even lectured him a time or two on his expectations being too far-reaching. He tipped his head and studied his friend.

"Has Mrs. King tried to match you with anyone?"

Norman shook his head. "Not as of late. I believe she gave up her quest sometime in the autumn if not before."

"Hmmm. Interesting." If he was remembering correctly, that was also right around the time when she began speaking more and more about her niece who was to join her in Bath.

"How so?"

"She is not the sort to give up on seeing someone well-matched. Heaven knows I have tried to get her to leave off matching me."

"That does make it interesting, but I am sure there was a reason."

Most likely, the reason was now living in one of Mrs. King's guest rooms, but he would not say as much to Norman. He would just bide his time while watching and listening – and scheming with Grace. He smiled.

"You do look exceptionally happy today," Norman commented. "But I guess knowing the lady you love returns that love will have that effect on a gentleman."

"Indeed, it will. I am going to Erondale as soon as I am through here. I thought it best not to arrive in my travelling clothes and famished." He swallowed the last of his tea. "Are you going to visit either Mrs. Shelton or Mrs. Clayton today?"

"I had not intended to do so, but I am free for the afternoon. A social call would not be out of the question."

"Then allow me to offer you a ride, though I do hope to convince Grace to go driving with me while you are occupied with the Claytons and Sheltons. So, I will not be available to cart you back to town for an emergency should one come calling."

"I am certain I can be free from being called away for a few hours, and if not, perhaps Clayton would do me the service of conveying me back to town." He rose from his place at the table. "And while you are driving me to Erondale, perhaps, you can tell me why you were in travelling clothes."

~*~*~

"I had hoped that what I had heard was not true," Norman said as they approached Erondale and Walter had finished telling him his tale of chasing after Ramsey once he had discovered that the man had left the Upper Rooms.

"What did you hear?"

"Just that Ramsey was seen with some pretty lady who was not the same pretty lady he had been dancing with at the ball, and that it seemed he was playing Miss Love false."

That was what it most certainly looked as if

Ramsey was doing. Walter shook his head and sighed. "Gossip travels quickly."

"Excessively," Norman agreed. "I do not carry it myself, but I am often privy to a great many interesting tidbits." He blew out a breath. "If there is one festering pustule that I would like to see eradicated, it would be the wagging tongue. Far too much damage can be done by one exposure to it. However, to this point, no one has discovered a tincture, tonic, or extraction procedure to rid society of the dread disease."

He was, of course, speaking from experience – grievously miserable experience. It almost made it understandable that the man would not wish to risk another exposure to such ruinous viciousness again even for a chance to gain the lady he loved.

Walter jumped down from the gig and waited for Norman to join him before proceeding to Erondale's door.

"We have been waiting for you," Roger said as he opened the door.

Where was the butler? Walter peeked behind Roger and saw Graeme.

"Is something amiss?"

Roger's grimace was enough of an answer to set Walter's heart racing.

"What is it?" he asked as he stepped inside the house.

"This." Roger held out a letter. "I told her that I would see you received it."

Her? With great trepidation, he took the missive from Roger. On the front was his name, very prettily written with a feminine flourish.

"Come. Have a seat before you read it," Graeme suggested.

"Is she gone?"

Graeme's nodded. "Have a seat. Read the letter. And then, we can tell you what we know."

Walter shook his head. "Where did she go?"

"Home," Roger answered.

"How long ago?"

"It was about seven this morning when they left."

Walter turned toward the door. "There is still daylight." He could cover a good bit of ground before it was dark if he left now. He might even be able to overtake them on the road if he travelled through the night.

Graeme grabbed his arm and steered him into

the sitting room. "Did you discover anything about Ramsey?"

Walter shook his head. Why did they want to know that now? There were more pressing matters needing attention. The woman whom he loved and who had said she loved him had left, and he needed to be away.

"Blakesley," Norman said, "please, take a seat."

"But Grace –"

"Left you a missive she wishes for you to read," Mrs. Clayton inserted. "There were a good number of tears that went into its writing. It would be a shame not to read it."

"And you cannot leave until you know where to look," Roger added when Walter hesitated and looked once more toward the door.

That was true.

"And we will not tell you that bit of information until you have had the rest of it."

Walter scowled at Roger and, then, took a seat as close to the door as possible. "Tell me what I need to know."

"Ramsey has left Bath," Graeme said.

"I know that. I followed him as far as I could."

"Did you know that Miss Love sneaked out of her house to go see Ramsey?" Graeme asked.

Walter's brow knit. "How would I know that?" He unfolded the letter he had been given. His curiosity would wait no longer to be satiated.

"You would not unless we told you, which is why you need to take a moment before running after Grace," Roger said. "We are not attempting to keep you from her."

Walter sank back in his chair as he read what Grace had written. "She meant to break off with me?"

"No," Mrs. Clayton said quietly. "She thought she was doing the proper thing."

Walter looked at her in confusion. "How is it the proper thing?"

Mrs. Clayton glanced at her companions. "Her sister might be with child."

"Ramsey's child?" Only Graeme did not look as surprised as Walter was at the news.

Mrs. Clayton nodded. "Why would any gentleman such as yourself wish to be tainted by such a scandal as Felicity has created?"

"Because he loves Felicity's sister."

Mrs. Clayton nodded again. "Love is also

Grace's reason, for because she loves you so much, she could not fathom allowing you to be discredited or harmed in any way."

"But her leaving me is the harm," Walter protested. A few whispers were nothing to him. It was not as if he had gotten Miss Love with child. That was Ramsey's cross to bear. "I will not allow her sister to take yet another gentleman from her – especially not one who loves her as fiercely as I do." He rose. "I need to know where I am going."

Chapter 19

Chickens fluttered their wings and squawked in the small patch of fenced-in garden next to a hen house while shouts from one servant to another lifted above the clatter of the courtyard below. Grace sighed and rested her head against the back of the rocker she had drawn from the corner of the room to the window.

It was lovely to be off the road again, and this inn was a touch nicer than yesterday's, but none of that truly soothed her as it would have on her trip to Bath. Several days on the road when anticipating adventure were much easier to endure than the same number of days spent travelling while one's heart was breaking.

She closed her eyes. A tear slid down her cheek, and she brushed it away quickly.

"Are you still so disappointed?" her mother

asked from where she sat at a table with her needle-work spread out. Felicity was flopped across the bed, and their father was below stairs, likely talking with some gentlemen at the bar.

Grace shrugged and nodded. She did not want to speak about it. She wanted to be miserable and alone. However, as it was, she was only allowed to be miserable. One was never alone when travelling for one was either in a carriage with her family or in a rented room with at least a sister.

She turned her head to the right until she could just see Felicity. She felt dreadful for her sister, of course, but she also could not bring herself to the point of completely forgiving her for her stupidity. Sneaking out to kiss a gentleman in a garden was one thing. Sneaking out to allow him to take you to bed was another altogether. It really did not matter to Grace how much her sister protested that Mr. Ramsey had proclaimed his love for her or how he had spoken of marrying. It was foolish. She would never sneak out to visit Walter at his home in such a fashion. Not even if she enjoyed his kisses and caresses — which she would never know as he had never kissed her.

She closed her eyes and tried to remember what

it felt like to be held by him as she had been at his townhouse with his strong arms encircling her while she rested against his firm chest.

Another tear slid down her cheek. How she missed him!

"We will have to begin planning for your season as soon as... well... soon." Her mother smiled tightly. What was to become of Felicity had been a topic of discussion today in the carriage. If all was well — meaning she was not with child –it might be reasonable to allow her to participate in some of the season's activities. Their mother was certain that some gentleman would be willing to take her on. There was no way for a gentleman to know that she was not a maiden as long as gossip did not follow her.

That was the biggest concern, for it seemed Felicity was incapable of not being followed by gossip. And if it did not follow her, she seemed to create it wherever she was. At school, she had been the topic of several stories that had circulated. Those had been mostly innocent. Miss Amelia Abernathy was a great lover of posing dares, and Felicity was all too willing to prove herself as fearless. However, those dares had been just for fun.

Nothing more than a day or two of discipline by the headmistress had been at stake.

"I do not want a season," Grace said.

"Not want a season? That cannot be. You will miss your friends for now, but, in a few months, you will forget the time with them which you were made to miss and will be eager to be on your way once again."

Grace shook her head. "I shall never forget." There was so much to miss!

Bea and Victoria had not yet told anyone else about their babies. Only Grace had been privy to their conversations about becoming mothers. Only she had heard their excitement and apprehension. She would miss that. It would not happen again.

And then, there was Walter. She did not need a season, for she had no heart left to give to any gentleman. Ever. She had not lied when she had written to him that her heart would never forget him. She sighed. Being in love was not so amusing as she had expected it to be. It was dashed hard to not put her own desires ahead of what would be best for him.

And that was why she was having a horrid time of forgiving her sister.

Her mother looked up from her work as she pulled her needle through the fabric. "You are not pining over Mr. Norman, are you?" There was a hint of a scold in her tone. "There will be far better choices in town next year."

"She does not love Mr. Norman," Felicity said from the bed.

Oh, dear! She had thought Felicity was asleep.

"Well, I am happy to hear that," her mother said. "He was a lovely fellow, but he was not for you."

"Yes, Mother. He did not own land," Grace replied flatly.

"There is that," her mother agreed. "But he was not right for you. You need someone far more... Oh, I do not know what the proper word is for it. You just need someone who is more... Well, to put a fine point on it, you need someone more like Mr. Blakesley. He is amiable and lively. I dare say you'd not want for enjoyment if you were to marry him."

There was more to her mother's complaint about Mr. Norman than just that he was a physician? Grace was surprised. It would have been nice if her mother had made such a thing known before now.

"Mrs. King said the same thing," Grace admitted. "I think that Mrs. King would like Mr. Norman to marry her niece. It was not said, but I think they would make a good match."

"Then, you are truly not attached to the man?" her mother asked.

"She loves Mr. Blakesley."

Grace froze in her chair. Perhaps if she sat very still her mother would not remember she was there, or perhaps someone could knock at the door and distract her mother. She wanted to peek at her mother for she was so silent, but she dared not.

"Mr. Blakesley?" Unfortunately, her mother had found her voice and no knock at the door had distracted her.

"She calls him Walter."

Felicity had barely spoken a word in the two days since leaving Bath. Could she not remain silent for just a bit longer?

"Does she?" Their mother sounded quite excited. Still, Grace sat perfectly still, not daring to make a noise or movement.

"I do not think she was ever truly being courted by Mr. Norman."

Oh, wonderful. Not only was Felicity not going to remain silent she was going to become astute.

"Was she not?"

From the sounds Grace heard, she imagined Felicity had propped herself up on the bed.

"Why would she pretend that Mr. Norman was her suitor?" her mother asked.

"I am sure I do not know," Felicity replied. "Why would you do that, Grace?"

"Do what?" Grace asked.

"Do not play stupid," Felicity retorted.

How she wanted to retort that it was not she but Felicity who was stupid, but that would not be kind nor would it aid her cause at the moment. She did not need her mother to be put out before she needed to be.

"Why would you pretend that Mr. Norman was courting you?" Their mother asked. "Turn your chair so we can see you."

Grace rose and did as instructed.

"Now, tell us why," her mother commanded once Grace had taken a seat.

"Because of Felicity." That was the entire reason

as shocking as it appeared to be to her sister, though it should not be.

"I do not understand," her mother said. "How could Felicity be the reason for your subterfuge?"

Grace sighed. "Felicity is always the reason. She is why I was not allowed to flirt with Mr. Everett Clayton. She was the reason why I was not to even consider Mr. Ramsey at the Abernathy's house party." She felt a pang of regret at having mentioned his name when her sister closed her eyes. "And she was the reason I had no season. She either gets or takes everything." Grace blew out a breath. "Therefore, I thought it best to keep Mr. Blakesley a secret from her so that she would not take him from me." She closed her eyes. "But as it turns out, she has taken him anyway." Tears once again slid down her cheeks while she attempted to dash them away before they were seen.

"Oh." Her mother seemed lost for words beyond that one word.

"I did not take him from you," Felicity protested.

Grace shook her head. "You are right. You took me from him. I suppose there is a difference, though the result is the same."

"How have I taken you from him? Because we

are going home? And you are no longer in Bath?" Felicity looked honestly confused. "Surely, he can call on you at home."

"In Kent? That seems a rather long drive for a call, do you not think?"

"I did not mean he would drive it all in one day. He could come for a visit. Father can invite him."

"No, he cannot. I have broken off with him."

"Why?" Felicity cried.

"Do you truly not know what you have done?" Was her sister really that senseless?

"No one knows what I have done," Felicity said through clenched teeth. "They only know that I was treated poorly by Mr. Ramsey."

"You were seen at his apartment. It does not take a great mind to decipher why you would be there." She blew out a breath. "And if there is a child..." She shrugged. "I could not ask Walter to be tied to such a scandal. His home is in Bath you know. He will not get to drive away from any gossip." Her words were cutting, and she knew it.

Felicity looked horrified. "Surely, you are being far more dramatic than the situation warrants."

"Not all families would approve of a connection to ours at present," her mother said. "Perhaps after the air has cleared for a time, then we can invite Mr. Blakesley to Kent." She gasped. "Kent! You said he had a lady in Kent." She gasped again. "You were speaking of yourself! Oh, you, sly girl!"

Grace had expected her mother to be more irritated and less pleased about having been duped. However, it was likely good to have one parent who was not utterly put out with her. Her father would not be as amused.

"You love him?" her mother asked.

Grace nodded. With all her heart.

"And does he love you?"

Grace thought once again about how he had held her in the drawing-room at his townhouse and how he had told her that he hoped to one day be able to offer for her. She thought about how delighted he had been when she told him she loved him in the corridor at the Upper Rooms, and how he mentioned speaking to her father. And then, he had told Mrs. King that she was from Kent. She smiled despite the pain each memory brought her.

He loved her. She was absolutely certain of that.

However, there was a knock at the door before Grace could push her memories of Walter away and answer her mother.

"I have brought a visitor," her father said as he pushed the door open slowly.

"Walter?" Grace cried. Were her eyes deceiving her? The gentleman behind her father looked a great deal like Mr. Blakesley.

"Mr. Blakesley and I have had a very interesting discussion."

It was him. He had come for her. She just knew he had.

"Grace." Her father's tone and look were stern. "I am not an advocate of deception, though I do think I understand the faulty reasoning behind it." He tipped his head and smiled at her. "Your deep disappointment in leaving Bath makes a great deal more sense now." He held out his hand to her. "I think Mr. Blakesley would like to have a private discussion with you, or, at least, as private as a discussion can be in the yard of an inn."

He wanted to speak to her privately! Her heart was surely going to burst from joy.

"Mr. Blakesley, I am entrusting you to make certain no other scandal befalls my family."

"I would never do anything to harm your daughter or her family," Walter said.

Grace sighed. He was so noble, so good, and so...

well... everything. Was there another man in all of England as perfect has Mr. Blakesley? She was certain there was not.

Mr. Love placed Grace's hand in Walter's. "I am excessively pleased to hear that." He winked at Grace. "I will wait here with your mother for the happy news." Then, he shooed them from the room and closed the door, leaving them standing in the hallway of the inn.

Chapter 20

Walter looked up the hall and then down. Seeing it was empty, he pulled Grace into his arms for a quick embrace – not long enough by half but enough to assure himself that she was truly there with him. Two days of travelling and stopping at inns in search of her had been two very long days.

"Do not ever leave me again," he whispered before releasing her. He grasped her face between his hands. "Promise me, you will not leave me." He pressed a quick kiss to her lips. Again, it was far from how he wished to kiss her.

"How can I promise that?"

There was a twinkle in her eye that spoke of her understanding full-well what he meant. However, there were also tears clinging to her lower lids. It was an apt picture of how he felt – a tumultuous mix of lingering pain from separation and sheer delight at having found her.

"Marry me. We can live at Erondale or in town. I do not care as long as you are with me." Her smile was welcoming. "Please, will you be my wife?"

Her lips parted as if she was going to speak and then they closed as she cast a look at the door in front of which they still stood. He took her hand and, tucking it into the crook of his arm, led her the short distance to the stairs which would take them to the public rooms below. He was certain he knew what or, more precisely, who was causing her to hesitate.

"I know about your sister. Your cousin told me." He drew her close and spoke in low tones. Not everyone in the establishment needed to hear what he was saying. But she did.

It was not a very far journey from the bottom of the stairs to the door. However, they did have to wait twice – once for a maid to enter a room with a tray laden with dishes and once for a fellow who required a cane to assist his bent form in walking.

"Then, you know why I left," she whispered after the man with the crooked back had passed them.

"Partly. Your parents required you to leave Eron-dale. However, they did not require you to leave me. That was your decision." He let her exit before him. The air outside was a bit fresher than it was within, but it was still not without its own blend of aromas – food being cooked mingled with dirt and dust, as well as the scent of animals. It was not where he would have chosen to speak to her about serious matters, but it was the best they were going to be afforded.

"There is a tree with a bench just behind the hen house," she offered

"Is there?"

She nodded. "I have been looking out the win-dow for some time wishing to be anywhere but in my room and had thought of asking to go sit there. It is not as lovely as the bench in your garden, but it reminded me of that... and you." She rested her head against his shoulder for a moment but then with a gasp, she straightened. "I forgot," she whis-pered.

"I think we could withstand a few curious glances. I would venture to guess that most do not know we are only courting. I do not think it will cause a scandal."

She sighed. "But my sister has."

"Most likely."

"She will be the talk of Bath when the gentleman who lives below Mr. Ramsey shares his story."

"He will not be sharing anything." When Mrs. Clayton had shared that bit of the tale with him before he left Erondale, he had decided to delay his journey by an hour so that he might have a frank discussion with the fellow.

"How do you know?"

"As it turns out, he has been looking to rent a nicer set of rooms. Ones which could be found in one of my establishments and which will be his if he keeps his silence."

He had told the fellow that he was looking for a new tenant since he was planning to marry and wished to prop up his coffers by filling a vacancy. When the chap had discovered who it was that Walter was marrying, he had smirked and said something a trifle out of step. He would not make that mistake again, or he would be out of a fine set of rooms and be required to meet Walter for an early morning boxing match. Neither were things for which the fellow wished.

"You did that for Felicity?" Grace's eyes were wide with surprise and filled with delight.

"No, I did it for you. I only care what happens to your sister as it pertains to how it affects you. She is not my responsibility."

If it were not for how her sister's actions might harm Grace, he'd not have cared if the gentleman shared his story with everyone he met. However, Walter could imagine just how grievously that would distress a kind heart such as Grace possessed.

He took a seat next to her on the bench beneath the tree.

"My window is that one on the right."

He looked to where she was pointing.

"Do you suppose we are being watched?" he asked in a whisper.

She giggled. "I suppose we are."

He lifted her hand to his lips.

"Mr. Blakesley, we are not to create a scandal!"

He chuckled. "We will not. I have only kissed your knuckles." He kissed her hand once again. "Now, you were telling me why you decided to leave me."

She tipped her head and looked at him. Once

again, tears filled her eyes. Mrs. Clayton had said the note was not easily written, and it appeared that even thinking about having written it was painful.

"I could not allow you to be harmed." She blew out a breath. "What would your family think of your marrying someone with a sister such as mine?"

"Frankly, I do not care what they think. You are not your sister, and they will come to understand that."

"But what about the people in Bath? You need to retain a certain reputation to be able to continue to do business as you have been." She grasped both of his hands and looked at him very seriously. "While sitting out a dance or two, I have heard how much you are admired. I should hate to be the cause of that changing."

"They will also admire you. How could they not?"

She smiled. "You are impossible! It is entirely probable that many would hold my sister's actions against me. That is how it works. If one daughter is a wanton seductress, then her sister is assumed to be the same."

He shook his head. "Not always."

"But often." She punctuated her words with an exasperated huff.

He loved how she revealed all of her emotions to him. He doubted she did so with her sister or her mother. He had seen her affect expressions in their presence. He had never seen her do so with him.

"I will give you that there are some who think as you have suggested, but anyone who is too blind to see the goodness in you, my dear, is not worth my time." For such a person was likely either intolerably stupid or thought far too well of themselves. Neither were the sorts of people with whom he enjoyed doing business, though sometimes it was required.

"You have also been seen with Mr. Norman," he continued, "and he is highly regarded. I think you are worrying unnecessarily." Her mouth popped open. "However," he hastened to say, "I would rather bear a thousand heinous whispers than one more day without you. Please, say you will marry me."

"But –"

"My life will only be miserable without you in it. I love you, Grace. More than life itself."

Her lips trembled. "And I love you the same. These past two days have been wretched. I knew I must not put myself first, but how I wished to do just that and demand to be returned to Erondale."

"Will you marry me, Grace?" She was taking an interminable amount of time to answer a simple question, but then, she had been trying his patience since before they met. It was one of the things about her which, while driving him to distraction, he loved.

Her head bobbed up and down. "If it will ensure your happiness, I will."

"And what of your happiness, my love?"

"It will be greater than one person is likely supposed to be granted."

He lifted her hand to his lips again. "I wish we were not being watched."

She sighed. "That is too bad, is it not?" Her eyes rested on his lips. "We did just become betrothed."

"I gave my word to your father."

She sighed but then brightened and, leaning forward, kissed him. "I did not give my word to my father, and he is likely put out with me as it is."

Walter shook his head.

"It is not how I wish to kiss you," she whispered.

"We are in agreement there." He stood and offered his hand to her. They should return to her parents before he found it impossible to keep his word to her father. "I will send an express to my father if your father will allow it. I should like for you to meet my family."

"I would like that." She once again rested her head on his shoulder for a very brief moment as they walked back to the door to the inn. "But are you not returning to Bath?"

"Not unless you are. I was not jesting when I said I had no desire to be separated from you again."

"But you have business, do you not?"

"Nothing of a pressing nature. Norman has agreed to be my go-between if one is needed, and even Shelton offered assistance. He seemed very eager to see me on my way to claim you as my own. Do you know why?" he added when she giggled at that bit of information.

"He has been attempting to help me make a match since the house party we attended last summer." She smiled up at him. "It seems he has finally done it."

"Since when did he become a matchmaker?"

"Oh, he helped Mr. Clayton make a match with Bea."

"He did?"

Grace nodded as she climbed the stairs ahead of him. "He paid Bea marked attention while he was at Stratsbury Park, and that is all it took for Mr. Clayton to realize how much he loved my cousin."

Walter shook his head and chuckled. He was not certain that causing another gentleman to be jealous was precisely being a matchmaker, but it did seem like something Roger would do.

"And then, while attempting to find a match for me, he found a match for Victoria."

The match had been himself! Again, Walter was not certain he would place that under the auspices of being a matchmaker.

"And now," Grace said as she gained the landing, "he has helped me find you." Her brow furrowed. "Actually, I found you on my own. He just helped me keep you a secret."

Roger had been a wonderfully negligent chaperone. Walter could not fault the fellow for that since it had worked so well in his favour. He offered Grace his arm, and together they walked down the corridor. Before knocking on the door to the

Love's set of rooms, he once again looked up and down the hallway, and, seeing they were alone, pulled Grace into his arms for a brief embrace and far-too-chaste kiss.

"How long until you would like to marry and return to Bath with me?"

She sighed as he lifted his hand to knock on the door. "We should likely ask Mother. She has not yet had the opportunity to host a wedding breakfast, and mine might be her only chance."

"Then," he replied with a smile, "we will let your mother decide, though I will not be pushed to wait longer than three weeks. I will eventually have to return to Bath." He knocked and waited for someone to answer rather than allowing Grace to open the door for him. "And," he whispered just before the door opened, "I will not, for any reason, allow your sister to come between us. Not for a dance nor for the distance between Kent and Bath."

Chapter 21

Three and a half weeks later, Grace found herself once again settling into a strange room. However, this room and all the others below and above her would soon become familiar for they were to be her new home until the summer when she and her husband – she paused a moment and sighed at the wonderful thought – would take up residence at Erondale.

She put the last item for her toilette on her dressing table and took one more happy look around the modest-sized room which was fitted with wardrobes and dressers, as well as her dressing table and a lovely yellow sofa and footstool.

How wonderful it was that she had been forced to come to Bath on her sister's account! She chuckled to herself. Things had certainly changed in the time since she had first arrived in Bath with her family.

"Are you finished?" Walter poked his head into their dressing room. "It most certainly looks as if you are."

"Everything is as it should be." Grace rose and crossed to the door which joined this room to the master chamber.

"I could not agree with you more." Walter pulled her into his embrace and captured her lips for a kiss.

Grace sighed and melded to him. She was married – excessively, delightfully married in every way – and to the most wonderful man in all of creation. Her heart threatened to rupture with its joy at the knowledge. Walter was hers and hers alone.

"We have guests," Walter whispered when finally, he broke away from their ardent kiss. "And as much as they are the understanding sort, I dare say they would not be pleased to wait for an hour for us to join them, even if I wish to be locked away in this room with you for at least that long." He gave her a quick kiss.

"How do we have guests?" Grace asked as she checked her appearance in the mirror while Walter straightened and fidgeted with his clothing. "I did not think anyone would know we had arrived back in town until tomorrow."

In the mirror, she could see his grin. "What have you done?"

He shrugged and shook his head. "It is a secret," he whispered.

Grace giggled and hurried to follow him out of the room. Catching up to him, she wound her arm around his, pulling herself close enough that a good portion of her body touched his upper arm. She would affect a proper distance when they reached the bottom of the stairs, but for now, she wished to be as close to him as she possibly could be. However, when they reached the bottom of the stairs before she could affect her proper distance, he set her aside.

"Stay right here. Do not move, and do not peek."

"Shall I put my fingers in my ears and close my eyes?"

"If you wish."

She smiled. "I do love surprises. Well, happy surprises, not the sort that took me back to –" His finger on her lips stopped her from talking, and she put her fingers in her ears and squeezed her eyes closed.

He removed his finger from her lips and replaced it with a kiss. "Stay right here," he whispered, pulling one finger away from her ear so that she could hear him. "Do you know how lovely you are?" He kissed her lips again after she shook her head.

She popped one eye open to look at him.

"I will tell you about it later," he promised.

Grace closed her eye and counted silently in her head as if she was playing hide and go seek. She had gotten all the way to one hundred and nineteen before she jumped when a hand was placed on her arm and once again, one finger was pulled away from her ear.

"We are ready," Walter said.

"Ready for what?" Grace batted her lashes at him innocently, causing him to chuckle.

"Feigned innocence will not work with me, Mrs. Blakesley. I know you are very good a scheming. The only way to discover this secret is to follow me."

"Anywhere."

"I could be leading you into danger," he cautioned.

Grace rolled her eyes. "You would never do that."

"Are you certain?"

She nodded. There was no one, absolutely no one, whom she trusted more than the man standing before her. "I trust you." She ran her hand down his arm before placing it in his hand.

His fingers twined with hers, and the two of them proceeded from the stairway to the dining room.

"Oh, my!" Grace cried when the door was flung open to reveal a room decorated for a party.

The table was laid with flowers and candles in the center and the finest china and glassware at each place. The sideboard was laden with several covered dishes, as well as serving bowls and decanters of wine. A footman and a maid stood one on each end of the sideboard, smiling in an understated fashion at their new mistress. And gathered around the table were the Sheltons, the Claytons, Mrs. King and Miss Chapman, and, of course, dear, dear Mr. Norman.

"I wrote to Norman," Walter explained when

the cheers and hardy congratulations, which had greeted them, had died down and everyone was taking their seats. "And he arranged it all."

"You are a very good friend," Grace said to Mr. Norman.

"Better than I likely should be," Mr. Norman replied with a grin.

"And not a killer at all," Roger inserted, causing Graeme to chuckle and Walter to explain their first secret meeting to Mrs. King and her niece.

Mrs. King looked shocked at first, but then, smiled. "I knew you were the perfect match for Mr. Blakesley from the moment I met you." She leaned toward the table and to her right, lowering her voice just a touch as if sharing a secret across the table with Grace. "He needed a lively wife. I have always thought so."

"And yet, all the ladies you presented to me were not lively," Walter accused.

"They were as lively as I could find. It is not my fault that they were not intriguing enough for the likes of you."

"There is likely not another lady in all of England as intriguing as Grace," Walter replied. "At least, there is not to me."

"That is as it should be," Roger said. "Now, my wife is interested in knowing all the details about your wedding."

"I am interested? I think it is my husband who is interested," Victoria said. "Not that I do not wish to hear it," she added with a smile. "We truly could not be happier for you."

"Here. Here," Graeme cried as the first dish of stew began making its tour of the table and finding itself relieved of its contents.

"Your parents must have been surprised when Mr. Blakesley appeared at your door," Bea said.

"Oh, very!" Grace replied. "My father was not pleased with my subterfuge but was understanding once I explained all that Felicity had done." It had saddened her father to hear about it. He knew that his eldest daughter could be demanding and prone to getting her way, but he had not known those tendencies had devolved into taking advantage of her sister's gentler temperament.

"What had Felicity done?" Mrs. King asked with interest.

"Oh! I should likely not say, but since I forgot that you did not know, I suppose I must tell at least a portion." Grace looked at Walter who nodded.

"Mrs. King will keep it to herself." He gave the lady a pointed look. "She would not wish to have any harm come to you."

"It goes without saying, does it not, Annabelle?"

"Most certainly," Miss Chapman agreed. Her eyes darted toward Mr. Norman, who, Grace noticed, was doing a fine job of ignoring the lady. "Gossip is dangerous, and I would never wish to be the source of harm to another."

Mr. Norman's jaw clenched, and his head shifted just a bit as if the words were a blow to him.

"I am happy to hear it," Grace said while giving both Mrs. King and Miss Chapman a reassuring smile. "I think we shall be great friends, and that might require sharing secrets with one another. It often does."

"Very true," Roger muttered with a chuckle.

"My Grace is fond of secrets," Walter added.

"Only secrets of the best kind!" Grace protested. "I do not like those which would damage." Her hands were resting on her lap and her chair was placed just right to allow her to bump her husband's foot with her own, and for her to touch his knee without being noticed, which made him smile. After sharing a secret look with Walter, she turned back to her guests.

"My sister is fond of courting." That seemed a polite and kind way to say it. "And it is her belief that the elder should marry before the younger sister." She pulled her bottom lip between her teeth to keep from smiling too broadly. While that might have been Felicity's belief, it had not been what had happened.

"I will assume that such things have caused a gentleman or two to have been snatched up by your sister when you might have been interested in them," Mrs. King said. "I am not without siblings with strong opinions either." She winked at Grace.

"Yes, she has snatched a few," Grace answered simply. There was not much else to say. Felicity had stolen a couple of gentlemen from Grace but not the one who mattered, the one who held her heart and had covered her hand, which lay on his knee, with his own.

"Well, it seems it has all worked out for the best," Mrs. King added.

"Indeed, it has," Walter said. "My parents and brother were happy to meet Grace and her family. We stopped there on our way to Kent."

He continued to ramble on about the estate and the improvements being made to the garden while Grace half-listened. She had enjoyed meeting his family. She could see where Walter had gotten his drive to do well. His father was similar to him in that way, as well as in appearance. His older brother was, Grace had discovered, only older by a few minutes, and while he was nearly an exact image of Walter, his personality was quite different. He was the quieter of the two.

Felicity had found Walter's brother to be a great source of entertainment. It appeared that to Felicity the surest way to get over a broken heart was to flirt with an unattached gentleman. However, Grace knew from the tears Felicity shed each night before sleep that what appeared to be true was not the truth. Her sister's heart was well and truly broken. No gentleman was going to fix it. Time would have to do that.

She sighed as she took a sip of her wine. She would likely get a letter in a few weeks informing her if Felicity was to have a season or a child. The thought was enough to pull a grey cloud over the festivities around her. She knew that what Felicity suffered was of her own doing, but it was still not easy to contemplate that her sister might be less than happy for the rest of her life.

"Has –" she stopped. She could not ask that.

"What is that, my love?"

She shook her head. "I was just contemplating someone I had seen several times at several soirees and had thought to inquire after him. It is nothing."

Graeme caught her eye and shook his head. So, Mr. Ramsey had not returned? That was sad indeed. How did a gentleman declare his love and promise marriage one day and run away from it all the next?

"Mrs. Love is an excellent hostess," Walter said, thankfully, drawing the conversation back to a safer subject. "The wedding breakfast will be the talk of Kent for some time, I should think."

It would be unless Felicity was with child. Then, that would be the focus of gossip. Their father had declared that he would not cover it up. There might be a time away during the summer at the seaside for the family, but his daughter, who had gotten herself into such a predicament by being secretive, would be required to deal with the whispers and looks if it came to that. The announcement had been met with tears from nearly everyone, including her father. It was only Walter who had not found it necessary to cry over the ordeal. That is not to say he was not sensible to the tragedy. He was. He was just not the sort to shed tears over such a thing, or so he said, though his eyes had glistened when holding Grace's hand and attempting to comfort her after that meeting. He truly was the best of men!

"Oh, yes! The cake was delicious. I have requested the receipt from my mother so that I can add it to my collection," Grace inserted when Walter began discussing the food which was served.

"And the bride was – is – beautiful, so all was as it should be," Walter concluded.

Their discussion fell to the news of the area after that and continued with plans for the future as they all looked forward to the summer.

"Well, Mrs. Blakesley, shall we take a walk in the square now that we have eaten?" Walter swallowed the last of his wine.

"Only if our guests wish to join us."

"Oh, we are not staying beyond the meal," Bea said softly, a faint pink staining her cheeks.

"No, indeed!" Mrs. King agreed. "Newlyweds do

not need a house full of guests on their first evening in their home." Again, she winked at Grace, who blushed but was happy to hear she would be alone with Walter.

"I do not see why you could not take a walk with us before departing," Walter inserted.

"Would you even know we were there?" Roger quipped.

"I might remember it when you took your leave," Walter replied.

"Bea is tired," Graeme inserted. "We took a stroll through the gardens earlier, so I think it is best to take her home for a quiet evening. I also happen to know that there is a book, which she is eager to read, waiting for her at Erondale."

Walter rose. "Do not let it be said that I shooed you out of my house without offering to be hospitable."

"Who would believe such a thing?" Mrs. King asked with a chuckle. "You will both come call on me soon, will you not? My cook has a fresh supply of apple cake." Her eyebrows waggled. "I do hope it is still enough to tempt you to join me on occasion for tea."

"We would come even without the offer of

cake," Walter assured her. "However, the cake is greatly appreciated."

One by one, their guests joined them in the corridor and said their farewells. Walter promised each that he and his wife would call on them soon. He was eager to be seen in society with Grace on his arm.

"You are well?" Grace whispered to Bea as her cousin gave her a hug before departing.

"Quite. I find I am still tired but far less likely to cast up my accounts. However, I am hungry. Constantly hungry. I doubt my dresses will conceal my expanding belly much longer."

"My brother might come for a visit," Graeme said when departing. "He is not enjoying his time in London so very much, so I invited him and Max to join us for a few weeks."

"That would be wonderful!" Grace cried.

"Yes, it should give my husband something to do." Victoria's eyes shone with merriment. "You know he is claiming he helped you make a match."

Of course, he was.

"He was a help," Grace said. "If he had not kept my secret, who knows how things would have turned out."

"I suspect," Victoria said with a glance toward Walter, "that the results would not be so very different from how they are now." She embraced Grace before her husband said his farewells, and then the house was quiet. Very quiet.

"Shall we take that walk in the square?"

Grace shook her head. "Maybe tomorrow."

"Then what do you suggest we do, my love?"

"There is a lovely view of the square from the sitting room if a remember correctly."

"There is."

"I think I should like to view it just as I did the first time." She moved toward the stairs but only took two steps up them before turning around to face Walter. "Only this time," she said in a whisper, "I should like you to kiss me while we are there just as I hoped you would last time."

"Would you now?" Walter's eyes were filled with amusement and desire.

Grace placed a hand on his heart and then slid it slowly up to his shoulder. "Very much." She moved her hand around to his neck and leaned toward him. "But that does not mean you cannot kiss me now as well."

"But everyone will know that you like me," he teased.

She shook her head. "I do not like you, Mr. Blakesley. I love you with every inch of my being from my head down to my soul, and I do not care who knows."

"That is just how I feel about you, my angel."

"Then kiss me."

And he did kiss her – on that step and each of the others up to the floor where their chambers were located.

"But the square," Grace protested weakly.

"It will still be there tomorrow." Walter opened the door to the bedroom and pulled her inside, where, once he made certain the door was locked, he spent the rest of the evening ensuring that all thoughts of squares or balls or sisters or anything other than her wonderful good fortune in being loved by him were impossible.

As the moon grew brighter while the shadows of the night deepened, Grace sighed and rested her head on her husband's chest above his heart and allowed her eyes to flutter closed, drifting off into blissful sleep, here in the safe embrace of the gentleman who had once happily agreed to be her secret beau.

Before You Go

If you enjoyed this book, be sure to let others know by leaving a review.

~*~*~

Want to know when other books in this series will be available?
You can always know what's new with my books by subscribing to my mailing list.
(There will, of course, be a thank you gift for joining because I think my readers are awesome!)
Book News from Leenie Brown
(bit.ly/LeenieBBookNews)

~*~*~

Turn the page to read an excerpt of another one of Leenie's books

Other Pens, Mansfield Park Excerpt

[Have you ever wondered what happened to Henry Crawford after *Mansfield Park* ended? How about his sister or Tom Bertram? What about his friends who were never at Mansfield Park? If you have wondered about such things, you'll want to read my *Other Pens, Mansfield Park* series, which mixes Jane Austen's classic characters with a cast of original ones in situations never found in one of Miss Austen's novels. Below is an excerpt from the second book in the series, *Charles: To Discover His Purpose*, a story about how Henry Crawford's rakish friend Charles Edwards finds his happily ever after while attempting to steal a kiss.]

CHAPTER 1

Charles Edwards squinted into the late afternoon

sun – it was an action that he could almost do without any discomfort. The swelling around his eye had subsided, and soon, the bruising would fade to a nasty yellow and then disappear. Until that happened, he would continue to take his rides by wandering from one street to the next rather than face the taunting and questioning looks he was guaranteed to receive in the parks.

While it was an excellent way to avoid censure from his peers, it was dashed boring trotting up and down streets without so much as a single friend with whom to converse. Had he earned his scars more gallantly, perhaps he would not feel the need to hide them. To have been injured in a boxing match or defense of some lady's honor would make his bruises more of a badge than a blemish. However, since everyone in town had likely read that blasted article in the paper, the raised eyebrows from overprotective matrons and giggles from their charges would be unbearable. And then, there would be the gentlemen. He shook his head. Had he received a blackened eye from Trefor Linton for actually doing something inappropriate with Linton's sister, Constance, his friends would just laugh and clap him on the shoulder before filling his glass with some libation at his club.

But, he had not been caught doing anything improper. In fact, it was much worse than just not being found dallying with a debutante. He had been attempting to be gallant. He would do his best not to be put in such a situation again! Honourable actions and favours to ladies who were offering none in return must be avoided, for they only led to broken noses, disgrace, and lonely rambles up less well-to-do streets.

"Mr. Edwards?"

Charles drew his horse to a stop just in front of a carriage that was standing at the ready to receive a lovely young woman. He had not bothered to take note of her since this was not the part of town where the finest flowers of the season resided.

"Miss Linton," he said doffing his hat. "Is Crawford with you?" He nodded to the carriage.

"No," Constance Linton replied with a smile, "though he very much wanted to be. It is just Evelyn and I."

His brows furrowed. Evelyn? The name sounded familiar.

"Miss Barrett," Constance clarified.

"Ah, Miss Barrett. Of course. How negligent of me to not remember." How had he managed to forget her name? He certainly had not forgotten her perfectly pink lips or lithe figure...the same figure that was exiting the house to his left. She was perhaps the most enticing creature he had ever met and never sampled.

"Oh!"

Miss Barrett's lips formed such a wonderfully kissable *o*.

"Mr. Edwards," she greeted with a small curtsey. "Are you here to visit Mrs. Verity and the children?"

His brows furrowed again. "Mrs. Who?"

"Verity," Evelyn repeated. "She runs this home for children." She motioned toward the house.

"I did not know this was a home for children." His left brow rose in question. "Why are you here? None of these children are yours, I would assume."

Her eyes grew wide, and she gasped. "We are not all as reprobate as you, Mr. Edwards."

He leaned forward, nonchalantly admiring her look of utter indignation. "Then, what, pray tell, are proper young ladies such as yourself and Miss Linton doing here?"

"Charitable work. You do know what that is, do you not?"

He chuckled. Miss Barret was not the sort to shy away quietly to her corner and leave him be. He liked that. "I have heard the term."

"But have you ever experienced it?" asked Constance.

He shifted his gaze to his friend, Henry Crawford's, betrothed. "No, not beyond what is expected on my father's estate."

"It's rather fulfilling," Constance replied. "Today, we taught some children their letters. It was remarkable, was it not, Evelyn?" She wore a look of sheer delight.

"And Linton approves of this?" Charles asked.

"Both he and Henry do."

Delight did not begin to describe the look in Miss Linton's eyes as she said the name Henry. One day, when he was ready to take up his mantle of responsibility, Charles hoped to find a lady who would look even half as happy saying his name as Miss Linton did at this moment.

"Trefor," Constance continued, "thought this would be a safe way to keep me occupied. My last scheme, you see, did not leave him favourably disposed to allowing me to find ways in which to make my life more interesting."

There was a mischievous gleam in both her eyes and those of her friend Evelyn. Curious, that. He had not expected anything akin to impishness from Trefor Linton's sister or any of her friends. Constance Linton was the most proper chit he had ever met, and he suspected, to be her friend, Miss Barrett must be the same.

"Is your eye feeling better?" Miss Barrett asked.

"It is, but I'll not be doing either of you any favours in the future," he replied with a smirk. "At least not unless I receive something better than a broken nose and a black eye in return."

"I can neither apologize or thank you enough," Constance replied.

She had apologized over and over and over again as she stood holding a compress to his eye in the Linton sitting room those many days ago. "I think you have said the words enough," he replied softly. "I merely jest." He would not have her feeling guilty for his injuries when it was not her doing which caused them.

Miss Barrett tipped her head as she looked up at him, a puzzled look on her face. Then, she shook herself and smiled. "We are expected at your house soon, Connie. Mother will be waiting."

"As will Trefor," she smiled, "and Henry."

Much to Charles's surprise, Miss Evelyn Barrett rolled her eyes at the tone her friend used to say Henry's name.

"Do not let me detain you. I would not wish to run afoul of any of them." He winked at Miss Barret. "At least, not until I am healed."

She gasped. "My mother has warned me about you, Mr. Edwards."

"As well she should," he replied easily. "I am dreadfully charming."

Constance had entered the carriage, but Evelyn, who remained on the street, laughed. "That is not how my mother said it." Her eyes sparkled with impertinence. Then, with a small curtsey of parting, she boarded her carriage.

Charles looked after her and tipped his hat as the door closed on those shining eyes and teasing smile. Oh, he could find great pleasure in evoking such a look from her on a regular basis. Not that he wished to spend great amounts of time with her. No, he was not the sort of gentleman to trot around behind a lady hoping for her to smile at him or laugh at his jokes. He danced; he flirted; and he stole kisses. He did not become attached. Attachments were dangerous. They led to marriage and, he fought the urge to shudder, responsibility. He was far too young for such things as that just yet.

Still, he wondered where she would be this evening and if there would be any dark corners into which she might be persuaded.

He blew out a breath. Hiding himself away from society was perhaps not the best idea in the world. It apparently was wreaking havoc on his well-ordered, carefree existence. A rogue such as himself did not stalk his prey. He simply looked for the opportunity and took it. Planning anything was far too much like being responsible. Rules, guidelines, ledgers, accounts, and all the rest that went with being a gentleman of standing belonged to his father, not Charles.

In front of him, the carriage stopped, a man jumped down, the door opened, and a pretty face peered out, looking back to where he was.

He nudged his horse forward as Miss Barrett waved him towards her.

"Do you require help?" he asked as he drew near.

"No, no, we are well. Connie and I were just

talking, and I thought as we were discussing how dreadful it is that you were injured on Connie's account that it would be charitable of us to offer you a place in the Linton's box at the theatre tonight."

Charles began to shake his head.

"Hear me out. Do not refuse until I have made my full request. And come forward more, I feel as if I am going to fall out of this door and onto the street."

Charles chuckled. This young woman sounded more like Linton's cantankerous Aunt Gwladys than a young lady of the ton. Most young ladies who presented themselves during the season went out of their way to appear demure to one and all – always.

"Do you scold everyone?" he teased as he did as she said.

If he had expected her to be offended, he was once again going to be surprised, for she merely smiled, batted her lashes, and replied, "No, I scold very few beyond my brother actually."

"So, I am special," he returned.

She shrugged. "Perhaps you are. Or perhaps I just find you as troublesome as Griffin."

"I think I will insist you find me special."

"Do what you will; it matters not one jot to me," she retorted.

Her words might have said she did not care, but her tone clearly said she was annoyed.

"As I was saying..."

"Before you began scolding." Charles smiled at her huff.

"Before I had to pause to give instructions."

Charles chuckled. "Continue. I shall not refuse until you have said your piece."

"Refuse? You intend to refuse?"

"Most likely. But, I have not heard your request in full, so I cannot be certain I am correct until I do. I have been wrong before."

Her brows rose, and her lips pursed for a moment as if she were holding back some retort.

"There will not be very many people in our box. If you slip in a side door or something and scurry up to the box, you will not have to have many people gawk at you."

"You think I am worried about being seen?"

"I would be if my eye were the colour of yours. That *is* why you are riding here and not in a more populated place, is it not? And, I have not seen you at any events since...well..." she pointed to her eye.

"I will admit that I do not relish the whispers." Why he felt he needed to admit such a thing was beyond him. He could come up with any number of reasons to be riding where he was and for not having been at any soiree she had attended. A smile slipped slowly across his face. "Have you missed me?"

"What?" She shook her head vigorously. "No. I just noticed that I had not seen you slinking from shadow to shadow."

"If you say so."

"I do." She scowled. "Now, will you be joining us? I am certain no one would be in the least put out if you did."

"How reassuring," Charles muttered.

"Please," Constance added from the interior of the carriage. "I do feel dreadful that you have been out of society. It must be terribly boring sitting at home instead of going out."

"Who said I was sitting at home?" He smiled a lazy, suggestive smile.

"Henry," Constance replied.

Blast! Did Henry tell her everything?

"Very well, I have been hiding away. Are you happy to know my shame?"

"Only if it means you will join us," said Miss Barrett.

"Can you not muster an ounce of sympathy?" he asked in surprise. Were not young ladies – especially those who did charity work – supposed to be compassionate?

She shook her head. "No. Not a morsel. While I am awfully sorry you were injured, I do believe you have escaped more times than you have been caught."

The lady might look like an angel, but she had a heart of ice. However, ice could be melted. In fact, it could be quite a marvelous lark to attempt to melt that ice.

"Very well, I will join you if you will but attempt to feel an ounce of pity for me."

The way her lips pursed with contained amusement was tempting. "A full ounce?"

"Yes." He moved closer to her door. "A full ounce." He repeated the words in a low, sultry tone – slowly and deliberately. Satisfaction curled his lips as he saw her pretty nibble-worthy neck rise and fall when she swallowed.

She licked her lips. "I shall make an attempt."

"Then, I shall see you at the theatre."

"Very good."

He chuckled at the uncertainty in her voice. Again, he tipped his hat to the closed carriage door and watched it drive away before continuing on his way home to prepare for an evening of entertainment – and a play.

Acknowledgements

There are many who have had a part in the creation of this story. Some have read and commented on it. Some have proofread for grammatical errors and plot holes. Others have not even read the story and a few, I know, will never read it. However, their encouragement and belief in my ability, as well as their patience when I became cranky or when supper was late or the groceries ran low, was invaluable.

And so, I would like to say *thank you* to Zoe, Rose, Kristine, Ben, and Kyle, as well as my Sweet Tuesday readers on Patreon and my blog, who followed this story as it developed and waited, as patiently as one might do, from one Tuesday to the next to read a new chapter. I feel blessed through your help, support, and understanding.

I have not listed my dear husband in the above group because, to me, he deserves his own special thank you, for, without his somewhat pushy insistence that I start sharing my writing, none of my writing goals and dreams would have been met.

Other Leenie B Books

You can find all of Leenie's books at this link
bit.ly/LeenieBBooks
where you can explore the collections below

~*~

Other Pens, Mansfield Park

~*~

Touches of Austen Collection

~*~

Dash of Darcy and Companions Collection

~*~

Marrying Elizabeth Series

~*~

Willow Hall Romances

~*~

The Choices Series

~*~

Darcy Family Holidays

~*~

Darcy and... An Austen-Inspired Collection

About the Author

Leenie Brown has always been a girl with an active imagination, which, while growing up, was both an asset, providing many hours of fun as she played out stories, and a liability, when her older sister and aunt would tell her frightening tales. At one time, they had her convinced Dracula lived in the trunk at the end of the bed she slept in when visiting her grandparents!

Although it has been years since she cowered in her bed in her grandparents' basement, she still has an imagination which occasionally runs away with her, and she feeds it now as she did then — by reading!

Her heroes, when growing up, were authors, and the worlds they painted with words were (and still are) her favourite playgrounds! Now, as an adult, she spends much of her time in the Regency world, playing with the characters from her favourite Jane Austen novels and those of her own creation.

When she is not traipsing down a trail in an attempt to keep up with her imagination, Leenie resides in the beautiful province of Nova Scotia with her two sons and her very own Mr. Brown (a wonderful mix of all the best of Darcy, Bingley, and Edmund with a healthy dose of the teasing Mr. Tilney and just a dash of the scolding Mr. Knightley).

Connect with Leenie

E-mail:
LeenieBrownAuthor@gmail.com
Facebook:
www.facebook.com/LeenieBrownAuthor
Blog:
leeniebrown.com
Patreon:
https://www.patreon.com/LeenieBrown
Subscribe to Leenie's Mailing List:
Book News from Leenie Brown
(bit.ly/LeenieBBookNews)